what's going to happen to me?

what's going

o happen to me?

a novel
by Barbara Berson

CHARLES SCRIBNER'S SONS | New York

With love and kisses to:
Kenneth, Seth, Elizabeth, and Benjamin

Scott, your father's moving out of the house," my mother called out to me as she heard me come into the den through the back door.

Once in the kitchen where I could see her face, a kind of awful feeling started creeping into my stomach, like it had gone all empty or something. I could tell by the way her jaw tensed she was upset so I didn't want to ask anything. My younger sister was sitting at the kitchen table with tears running down her face.

"Your father's upstairs packing," my mother said. "We've decided that it would be best if he didn't live in this house anymore."

I shouldn't have been too surprised because

my parents had been fighting with each other like crazy for years. He was always hollering at her, saying that he wasn't coming back and then stomping out of the house and into his car and screeching out our driveway at top speed.

When I was a little kid I used to get real upset about his getting sore like that. So I would start to beg my mother to go after him. I always felt scared that he wouldn't come back. I believed what he said. But he always did come back. She always said he'd be back. She always told it like it was. That's why I knew that my dad was really going for good this time.

Inside I felt just like when I was a little kid, all scared and teary. There was a hot coal burning in my stomach. I couldn't think of anything to say or do so I just stood there looking at my mother and listening to the sound of Lisa's sobbing. I wanted to cry, too. We stayed just like that for a long time, it seemed. And that's how we were when my dad came into the kitchen with his suitcases in his hands.

"Well, Scott, I guess your mother told you the news." He had that tight look on his face, like when he got really sore about something and was ready to explode.

I nodded. I knew that if I tried to say anything I'd end up crying just like Lisa. I turned to my mother for help but her back was toward me. She was acting very busy washing dishes in the sink. I didn't know what I was supposed to say.

When my dad's voice broke the silence I was almost happy.

"Where's David?" he asked.

David's my older brother and even though we share the same room we don't do very much together.

"I don't know. I just got home from school," I told him.

Then my mother said, "David's upstairs in his room." Her voice sounded tired and when I looked at her back I could see her shoulders looked kind of droopy. I was wondering what I should do next when she said, "Go get him, Scott, so he can say good-bye to your father."

It sounded real funny to hear her say *your* father like that. It was like I had become divided somehow. Like I wasn't their kid anymore and didn't belong to the both of them or maybe it was my father who didn't belong to all of us anymore . . . I was beginning to feel mixed up somehow. It didn't feel good.

I ran out of the kitchen, relieved not to be in there with them. It scared me to see my mother like that, so uptight and quiet. She looked . . . different. It was scarier than when she and dad would be hollering at each other. Now there was all that silence and my father standing there with his eyes filled with tears. *I feel rotten,* I thought. My stomach was aching bad.

As I climbed the steps leading to the bedroom I wished silently that I had not come home so early that day. *If only I had stayed with Pete and played some more soccer after school he might have been gone before I got back,* I thought angrily.

"Dave," I called out as I reached the door of our room. "Dad's downstairs and wants to say good-bye to you."

Dave's head was bent over a book on his desk. He didn't move. Finally, as I neared his hunched-over shoulders, he looked up at me.

"Dave, didn't you hear me?" I asked. "Dad is leaving and wants to say good-bye."

"I don't care," he answered gruffly, not moving from his seat.

"Aw, come on, Dave. Don't be a pain. He's waiting." I was afraid of what might happen if Dave wouldn't come downstairs with me.

"I don't want to talk to him. I'm busy doing my homework," he said, giving me a sharp and unexpected poke in my hip with his elbow.

"Hey, that hurts." Dave's elbows were so boney that when he hit me with one I felt like I had been hit with a spear or something. Anyhow it hurt like hell. There was no time to start making a fight of it because just then we both heard my mother's voice coming up at us loud and clear. There was no fooling around when she sounded like that.

"Boys, come downstairs, this minute!"

Dave knew when she meant business, too. He began to slowly pull his long boney body up from his chair. *Jeez, he sure is tall and there isn't a drop of fat on him anywhere,* I thought, half admiring and half hating him. I always felt short and stocky next to him even though there was no reason. I was taller than most of the guys I knew, except for Jeff and maybe one other. And I sure had nothing but pure muscle on me. Even so, Dave, with those long arms and legs of his, could just put out that big paw of his and hold me at bay. There was no way I could reach him. The only time I could really get to him was when he didn't expect it. I'd get in there, right up close. Then I had a chance, except if I got jabbed by one of those pointed elbows of his.

The thing that really made Dave a great fighter was that he always looked so cool. He never looked scared or angry or anything. He'd just kinda grunt a little and *pow.* When he hit me, I knew it. I had to respect him. Everyone else did, too.

Like here we were going downstairs to say good-bye to our old man and there wasn't anything on Dave's face. I couldn't tell from looking at him that our whole world was cracking up. Not him.

"Dave," I whispered, "I hope he doesn't make a big deal out of this thing."

"Shut up," he commanded me, in his usual older brother tone. He seemed to know what he was doing so I decided to watch what he did and do the same thing.

I let Dave go into the kitchen ahead of me. This was one time I was glad he was bigger than me. This was one time being invisible would have been great.

"Well, boys," my father began, his voice beginning to crack, "I'll be in touch with you."

He shook Dave's hand and then he went for mine. I was very uncomfortable shaking hands with him. It was like he really wasn't my father but some polite stranger who was saying good-bye. I wondered if he would ever be like a real father to us again, now that he wasn't going to live with us anymore . . .

I wanted him to hug me, even though he hadn't done it for years. Somehow I didn't feel very grown-up right then. I guess it was a good thing that he didn't do it though because my eyes had begun to fill up with tears and I didn't want to act like a jerk. Instead, I shook his hand and swallowed hard, forcing the tears back down my throat. My sister, Lisa, was still wailing loudly, her tears dropping all over the kitchen table. She could cry all she wanted, and usually did.

My dad made a grab for her and pulled her out of the kitchen chair and started hugging her real tight.

"I don't want to leave you," he said to her, but I could tell he meant all of us, even my mother.

It was a gross scene. I stood there by Dave's side wishing the floor would open up and I'd be able to disappear into it. My mother just stood with her back tight up against the sink cabinet, her hands clenched at her sides. She watched my dad like she was a tiger ready to pounce. It reminded me of the jungle movies I used to watch on TV when I was a little kid. There were the hunters stalking the tiger on one side of this tall grass. Then the camera would switch to a shot of the tiger practically on top of the hunters but hidden by the same tall grass. It would just be standing there with all its muscles tensed and waiting, ready to jump if the hunters came one step closer to it. That was my mother right then. It was hard to tell whether she was scared or angry.

"All right," she growled. "That's enough."

My dad looked right at her, but kept hanging on to Lisa, who was beginning to sqirm around like she wanted to have him let her go. She was kind of short so that with my dad squeezing her against him the way he was she must have had a hard time breathing. At least she had stopped crying though.

"You're not going to be leaving the country, you know. You'll be able to see the kids whenever you want," my mother said.

She sounded just the way my English teacher talked when she was telling one of the guys to stop disturbing the class.

A sad beagle look came over my dad's face. He let go of Lisa, who looked positively relieved. Then he sort of took a step toward my mother. The look on her face changed suddenly and I really got scared. I could tell something really bad was going to happen. I wanted to stop my father but instead I found myself stuck where I was. I couldn't even say anything. It was like I wasn't really there, not my body anyway.

"That's enough," my mother said, stopping my dad from coming any closer to her. My dad just stood there like he was playing statues and my mother was the one giving the commands. Inside my head I knew this was no game. My mother wasn't playing. She seemed to be holding her breath, trying to figure out what to say next.

"Please go *now*," she finally said to him. Every word had to cut through the thick layer of silence that separated my dad from the rest of us—like the room was all closed against the sound of my mother's voice. It was like I was watching the end of a really scary movie. My chest was all sucked in from holding my breath.

My dad looked at her real hard. Then he moved. He turned around and walked over to where he had left his bags.

"Okay, then," he said, as he picked them up from the floor. He announced, "I'm leaving," as though his throat was hurting him and he could hardly make himself talk.

"I'm leaving," he said again.

None of us said anything as he went out of the room and into the den. I couldn't have, not if I wanted to keep those tears from pouring out of my eyes. I figured I knew just how my dad's throat must have felt because mine was burning from the salt in it just then, too.

We heard the back door close.

My mother moved after the sound reached us. We all followed her, like we had to know what she was going to do so we could know what we were to do. She went right up to the closed back door and turned around. She looked at all of us, one by one. Her back was resting against the door. For a moment there was no expression at all on her face. I felt awful tired, like I had played that soccer game after all. All my muscles were aching as though I had taken a hell of a beating on the field.

It seemed like ages since I had come home from school but I could tell from the sun still shining in through the back door window that it couldn't have been very long. It only felt that way.

I wanted her to say something, do something. Instead, she just stood there looking at us almost like she had never seen us before. We stood there watching her. We heard my dad rev up his car motor and then back down the driveway. We could always tell when he drove past the house and out into the street. This time it was different. There was no screeching of wheels. This time he didn't rush by us. It was like he was taking it slow and easy for a last look at the house.

I guess he was thinking about us, too. I was

just beginning to wonder about where my dad was going when my mother gave out a big sigh. She looked at all of us again but this time her mouth didn't look so tight and her eyes knew us.

"He's not coming back." She had a little smile on her face when she said it, kind of like she was sad and happy at the same time.

One thing was for sure, though—if she said he wasn't coming back it had to be true. She always knew about things like that. Somehow I didn't feel sorry about that. In a way I was almost glad he was gone.

My stomach stopped burning, and I was able to take a good hunk of air into my lungs. I could feel the tightness in my body slip away.

Later on, we all ate a quiet dinner. Afterwards, I went upstairs to do my homework. It was then I started to think about what had happened. I began to wonder what happened to kids who didn't have their fathers around the house. I remembered a TV show I saw one time about a kid who had no father around. He sure had some terrible things happen to him. Of course, I was no little kid anymore and I knew that was just a TV show. But all the same I just couldn't help wondering then about what was going to happen to me.

*T*he next morning when I got out of bed my stomach didn't feel too good. I didn't feel hungry, or like going to school either. I had crazy dreams all night and when I tried to remember what they were about they kept slipping away. It was like being teased. They were the kind of dreams that left me feeling awful tired and really down but glad it was morning.

I had tried to talk to Dave about our folks after we turned out the lights and were in bed. That's the time when we usually have some great talks. But he had just clammed up. Then I finally got out of bed and went over to him to start a fight the way we do when he's being stubborn.

He just punched me half-heartedly and said, "Aw, shut up and go to sleep."

I let him alone then and went back to my own bed, hitting my shin on the damn metal thing that stuck out from under my bed. It supported the bed or something, so I couldn't get rid of it even though my whole leg was almost busted up every time I walked around the room in the dark. I got back into my bed rubbing my shin because it was hurting like hell. Even that couldn't stop me from thinking about my folks.

It sure had been a rotten night. And it looked like it was going to be a rotten day. I had already slept through my alarm and could tell I was going to be late for school.

When the alarm went off Dave didn't even wake me up even though he was right there getting dressed. I complained to him because he let me sleep through the alarm but he said, "That's your problem. I've got no time to play around with you." He really thought he was tough.

"Scott, hurry up or you won't have time to eat breakfast," my mother hollered up to me.

I wanted to mumble something back like, "Who cares," but I didn't. Instead I called out that I was coming and made a beeline for the bathroom to wash up and comb my hair. I shoved the comb through my hair and looked at my face in the bathroom mirror. *It's bound to be a lousy day,* I told my face. I hadn't done my homework and that would really make it positively bad for me. *Mr. Schmidt will really lay it on me when I come in without my algebra assignment.*

I felt sick inside. I stuck out my tongue and studied it for a while wondering if it looked bad enough to convince my mother to let me stay home. My mother was rough when it came to cutting school. I wondered if I had a fever. I was really feeling sick, no kidding. There was that burning pain in my stomach . . .

"Scott, what are you doing up there?" my mother called up to me. She sounded like she was getting sore.

I stuck the comb into my back pocket and headed downstairs toward the kitchen.

They were all sitting around the kitchen table like nothing ever happened. Dave was jamming his breakfast into his mouth just as fast as usual. My mother was sipping her cup of tea. Lisa was buttering her toast.

"What do you want for breakfast?" my mother asked, looking up at me from her chair.

"Aw, I'm not hungry," I said, hoping that she'd ask me if I felt sick. Instead she said something she never said before.

"Well, why don't you just make some instant breakfast drink today?"

Jeez, things are really going to be bad, I thought. *She doesn't even care if I eat breakfast.*

I went over to the cabinet above the sink and got out a glass for the breakfast drink.

I figured that if she didn't care that I didn't want any breakfast there wasn't any use my trying to convince her that I was too sick to go to school. *Today's gonna be a real dog*, I said to myself.

"Don't forget to take out the garbage barrels before you leave, Scott," my mother told me as I opened the refrigerator door to get the milk.

"I'm gonna be late for school."

"You should have gotten up when your alarm clock went off," my dear little sister said.

"Dave could have gotten me up, except he stinks," I answered, glaring at Dave's back.

"That's not his responsibility, Scott," my mother said. The day wasn't getting any better.

I started pouring milk over the chocolate powdered stuff I had put into the glass. I was stirring the junk together when Dave started to speak.

I stopped banging the spoon inside the glass so I could hear him.

"Ma," he said, "now that dad's not living here anymore what are we going to do about our allowances and stuff like that?"

"Will we have to move from here?" Lisa piped in before my mother got a chance to answer Dave. "When Janey Nolson's parents got divorced her mother had to move them out of their house because they couldn't afford to live there anymore."

"Shut up, Lisa, and let ma answer Dave, will you?" I almost shouted. Lisa was a pain in the neck all right. She always tried to act so grown-up, but if I tried to do anything, like go into her room, boy, she'd start screaming like a real baby. She could hit me all she wanted but if I so much as gave her a little poke you would've thought I murdered her.

"Well, ma?" Dave insisted.

I watched my mother sip her tea slowly. I could tell she was thinking about her answer. She must have been having a hard time figuring out what to say because she sure took long enough before she answered. Actually, she really didn't give us any kind of answer after all.

"Well, right now I really don't know what's going to happen. It all depends . . ." she said, which left us all just hanging in there still not knowing anything. So I wanted to know more.

"On what . . . what does it depend?" I asked, looking around at Dave to see if he was with me. He was nodding his head. I guess he was pretty worried, too, even though he wouldn't talk to me about it. I felt better somehow knowing that Dave wasn't so different from me after all. He could feel scared and worried, too.

"Scott, I just don't have any answers for you right now," my mother said, frowning like I did when I couldn't figure something out.

"When will you know?" I insisted. I went over to the kitchen table with the glass in my hand. I sat down on the chair right opposite her. I didn't want to miss hearing anything.

"I guess I can't say anything definite until after we find out what your father can afford to pay for your support. I'm going to see if I can get a job . . . That won't be easy to do," she said, talking slow and looking more worried with each word. "I just don't know how everything will work out. That's all I can tell you right now."

Dave got up from the table and put his dishes in the sink.

"You know, ma," he said real slow, like he usually talked. He did what my ma was always trying to make me do. He always thought before he ever said a word. "Just because you and dad can't stand each other we kids shouldn't have to suffer."

That was just like Dave. He wasn't afraid of anybody. He could really lay it on the line. It was funny about him. He didn't talk much but when he did everybody seemed to listen to him.

I wanted my mother to know that I agreed with Dave so I added, "Yeah, we're not getting the divorce, you are. So why should we have to give anything up?"

"That's enough. I don't want to hear another word from any of you." My mother got up from the table and you could see she was burning mad.

"But ma," I started in again. Like usual, I couldn't keep my mouth from shooting off.

"I don't want any more talk about this today. Do you hear me?" I heard her and felt rotten. Her voice was raspy like she was going to cry any second. I guess she didn't want us to see how upset she was because she turned on the sink water and started making noises with the dishes.

Dave went out of the kitchen and through the den. In a second or two I heard the back door slam shut. Dave could always keep his mouth shut. I tried hard but somehow I never could.

I walked over to the sink. She turned her head to look at me.

"You'd better get off to school now, Scott," she said in a kind of whisper. Her eyes were all watery.

I decided I better get going like she said because I had a funny feeling that this was one time I would be really sorry if I stayed around.

Lisa was still drinking the last of her milk as I squeezed past her chair on the way out of the kitchen to the den.

I put on my jacket and picked up my books. For the past couple of years of school it seemed as though the books had gotten awful heavy. There were so damn many of them. I was always losing track of one or another of them. I'd left my algebra book over at Pete's the day before, which was another reason I didn't get my homework done.

I went back into the kitchen.

"I'm going now," I announced, still hoping way back inside my head that my mother would see I was too sick to stand up, let alone go to school that day. While I stood there waiting for her to notice me Lisa got up from the table and carried her dishes over to the sink.

"Ma," she asked, "can I tell Amy and Cathy about daddy's leaving?"

The coal in my stomach started burning real hot then.

"Yes dear," my mother answered, bending down to give Lisa a kiss on the cheek. "There's no reason why you can't tell your friends."

Lisa left then, smiling happy as could be. I wasn't happy though. I didn't want my friends making any cracks about my folks.

My mother turned off the water and faced me while she dried her hands on a towel.

"All right, Scott, what's the problem?"

"Aw, I don't know," I said, feeling embarrassed and stupid all of a sudden. "I guess I just wanted to know what's gonna happen to me?"

She walked across the kitchen to where I stood and put her arms around me. It was queer, because I was a couple of inches taller than her and she had to pull my head down to kiss me.

"Don't worry, baby," she said, "everything will be just fine. I promise."

She held my face between her hands and looked right into my eyes. You could tell she meant it. I believed her.

"Now get to school." She turned me toward the doorway and gave me a pat on my backside like when I was a little kid leaving for kindergarten or something.

I heard her call out the back door behind me, just like always, "Have a good day, dear."

By that time I had left our yard and was on

the way toward Pete's house. He lived just around the block from us. Usually I took a shortcut through our neighbor's backyard and got to his house pretty quick.

Today, I took the shortcut but I didn't feel like rushing. I kept remembering that first period was my algebra class. I didn't think I could make it through the day. I knew that I was very sick. *Maybe the school nurse will send me home*, I wished, but I knew I was only kidding myself. She was worse than my old lady when it came to things like cutting school.

"Hiyah, Scott," Pete hollered from his back steps. He was sitting there with his crazy long scarf wrapped around his neck. One of his sisters had made it for him.

Pete was a funny guy. He wore the nuttiest clothes and pretty soon everybody else was doing the same thing. You couldn't help copying him because he made everything he did into some kind of a wacky adventure.

"You'd better move it or we'll be late for school," Pete said. "I'll be killed for sure if the office sends another late note home to my parents."

"I'm coming," I yelled back, running. I didn't feel like I wanted to have any words from my homeroom teacher today. She could be a real bitch if a guy came in late to class, even just two minutes late.

"What took you so long?" Pete said, swatting me over the head with his notebook.

"Hey, that hurts," I shouted in pain, socking his books out from under his arm onto the sidewalk.

"Y'know, if you keep horsing around like this we're gonna be in for big trouble," Pete warned me as he bent down to gather up his books.

"Yeah, I know. But I don't really care," I mumbled under my breath as I bent down to help gather up Pete's papers which had begun to scatter in the early fall wind.

"Hey, here's your algebra book," Pete said, handing me a book that lay on the ground to his right. "How come you didn't come over last night for it?"

"Aw, I couldn't get out of the house," I told him.

"Why, you been grounded or something?"

"Naw . . . something else . . ."

"What's up?" Pete finally asked, looking at me kind of curious.

"Well, you remember the stuff we've been talking about lately?"

"Yeah?" he answered with a question, telling me he didn't know what I was talking about.

"You know, my folks and their fights."

"Oh that." He looked a little brighter, like he understood me all of a sudden.

"Yeah . . . well . . . well. They split up." I said it real fast. Like I had to get it out of me in one shot.

We were walking down to the end of the

block. The morning business traffic was pretty heavy. We stopped on the curb waiting for a break in the flow of cars.

"Whatdya mean, your folks split? What happened?"

"Come on, let's make a run for it." I hollered as I saw the break we were waiting for. It was like that every morning. Sometimes we would try to chicken the drivers out by running slow enough to make them think they might hit us.

"Boy, what a chicken. Did you see him slow down?" Pete laughed. He had a great laugh. It was almost a roar and it was funny coming out of him because he wasn't a big guy. But the sound of him laughing always broke me up even when I didn't think it was all that funny.

We began walking faster. Pete's scarf flew out behind him like a kite. He would wear that scarf practically all year long, except for the summer when it was real hot. Then he would walk around town almost naked, no shoes or shirt. He was a crazy guy.

"Did they have a big fight or something?" Pete asked. "Is that why they're splitting up?" His breath was coming out in short little gasps. He really had to work hard to keep up with me. Besides having shorter legs, he sure was no jock.

"They just split, dummy, that's all. My father packed his things and left the house for good yesterday." Pete could sure be thick when he wanted.

"Y'mean they're gonna get divorced or something?"

"Yeah, I guess so," I answered, relieved that it finally was out. I felt dumb telling anybody about it, even Pete and he was my best friend. I turned to see if he was looking at me funny.

"So what's your problem?" Pete asked, not looking at me but down at the ground in front of him.

"Aw, I don't know. It's just all so crazy. My mother doesn't know anything. We ask her questions and all she can do is say she doesn't know. It's nuts. Like I don't even know if I'm gonna get an allowance anymore. Stuff like that." I was glad to talk now. Pete was listening too, like he really understood and cared about what I was telling him.

"Aw, it's not such a bad deal," Pete said, when I finally stopped shooting off my mouth. "Lots of guys have parents who are divorced and they're doing all right."

"Yeah, like who?"

I could see the front door of the school and it looked like everyone was inside already.

"Hey, come on. We're late." We started walking faster.

"Y'know Keith?" Pete said.

"Yeah, sure, so what about him?" I asked, not really caring. I was thinking about what I knew I would get when I walked into my homeroom class. *Jeez, I wish Mrs. Schlosskind's absent today.* I started really pushing my feet. I didn't want to catch hell for coming late to class. This was one day I didn't think it would be funny to watch Mrs. Schlosskind's fat, red face turn purple.

"Keith's parents are divorced." Pete's words stopped me.

"I didn't know his parents were divorced. Is that why he ran away from home last winter?" I asked.

"Yeah, I guess so, but he got back home after a couple of weeks and everything turned out just great for him."

"That's funny. I always wondered why Keith's father was never at home." I thought about Keith and the times I was over at his house. There was always just his mother and grandmother hanging around. Keith never mentioned his old man to me. "I kinda thought his father was dead or something," I told Pete.

"Naw, his father's alive. When his folks first split up Keith used to go hunting and fishing with his old man. His father's some kinda outdoorsman type. At least that's what Keith told me about him."

"Yeah?" I said, wondering if my dad would ever want to do something like that with me. He never did go for that stuff when he lived with us . . . maybe now though . . . *Hmmm,* I thought to myself.

"Yeah, whenever he talks about his dad it sounds like he thinks he's the greatest. But, man, does he ever hate his mother," Pete continued.

"How come he lives with her then?" I asked.

"I don't know. I guess he has to. The law or something."

"That sounds shitty," I said, my stomach beginning to ache again.

"Yeah, I guess so . . ." Pete said, sounding like he didn't really care one way or the other. "But you know that stuff you were worrying about?"

"Y'mean like getting an allowance?" We'd reached the school by then and we stood for a second outside the entrance door.

"Yeah, like that. Keith has a great deal going."

"Like what?" I asked, wondering about how great a deal anybody could have if he had to live with a mother he hated.

"He gets two allowances out of it."

"How does he manage that?"

I pulled on the handle of the front door. It opened up and we started into the building as Pete answered.

"Well, Keith told me that since his folks don't talk to each other they never find out that the other one is already giving him his allowance. Isn't that a blast?"

We laughed all the way down the hall to our homerooms.

Even Mrs. Schlosskind's dirty looks didn't bother me so much now that I was busy figuring how I could work on my folks for two allow-

ances. *Jeez!* The thought suddenly hit me like the soccer ball smacking full speed into my belly, knocking out all my wind. *What if I can't get any allowances, from either one of them? What would happen to me then?*

A lot of weeks had passed since my dad had left our home. At first it was kind of funny not seeing him around. Like the house seemed emptier or something. But at least things were peaceful for a change. There was no more of that hollering and fighting around dinner time except if my dad happened to call us on the phone.

My dad kept asking me questions about stuff I wasn't supposed to talk about. Like, what was my mother doing? Was she treating me all right? Things like that. If my mother got wind of what he was asking she just blew up and started screaming at me for talking too much. It got so it just wasn't worth the hassle . . . talking to my dad, I mean. Like every word I said to him was wrong.

I was walking with Pete to the shopping center. It was about six blocks from my house. I was thinking about how things had changed for me. It kind of made a guy wonder about life and the future. I was pretty worried and told Pete about how I felt. After we talked about it I felt better. It made some of the tightness inside my head go away.

Pete was a good guy to talk to about deep stuff. He read an awful lot. I guess that's why he could always come up with something somebody wrote on just about any subject I could think of. Pete told me Shakespeare wrote, "Life is a stage, and people were only actresses and actors." I had to respect Pete for knowing so much, although sometimes he acted like his brains had gotten lost when it came to anything that he didn't like.

"Boy, it sure stinks," Pete said. It took me a second or so to connect because my mind wasn't with it right then.

"Yeah? What stinks?" But I already figured out what he meant.

After talking to my dad the night before I had called up Pete and told him the bad news.

"You, having to go get a job. That's gonna ruin everything. Why are your folks so cheap?" Pete really meant what he said.

"It's not that." I was beginning to get sore at Pete for mouthing off about my folks. They weren't the greatest, but there were worse. "My folks just aren't as rich or as dumb as Keith's," I told him. "Even my mother had to go out and get a job . . ."

But I knew what Pete was thinking about. He was remembering how tough my folks made it for me even before they split up. To get my ten-speed bike I had to save up for more than a year till I could get up the amount I needed. Sure my folks gave me half the amount I needed, for a birthday present, but I had to get the rest of the money myself.

"Y'know your parents have to take care of you. You're still under age. You ought to tell them that!" Pete knew about things like that because his old man was a lawyer.

I could understand why Pete was sore, but I didn't like his pushing it down my throat. I wasn't too happy about it myself. After all, what guy in his right mind wouldn't like fooling around with his buddies after school instead of having to be all hung up working and with no free time. I figured my life was just about ruined but there wasn't much I could do about it, no matter what Pete said.

"My folks sure wouldn't ever do that to me," Pete said, making me feel like breaking his neck.

"Listen, dumbhead, just 'cause your folks are loaded you think everybody is."

Pete didn't answer me. He knew what I meant. I watched him put his hand into his rear pocket and finger his wallet. He had over fifteen

bucks in there. He'd shown it to me when he came over to pick me up. He had no trouble getting money, or anything else for that matter. All he had to do was ask somebody in his house for something. He was the baby brother and all his sisters and brothers let him get away with murder. *I guess being the baby in a family really pays off good.*

I was thinking how my kid sister was the only one in my family who wasn't going to have to worry about money. She was too young to be able to earn any money. So she was getting an allowance. What made me sore was when I was her age I had a newspaper route. I didn't see why my folks didn't make her go out like they did Dave and me.

"Maybe your mother would pay you if you worked around the house or something." Pete was still pushing. The guy was beginning to bug me.

"Jeez, don't you understand anything? My dad just can't afford to pay my mother enough for our support. She just hasn't got enough to dish out extra money for anything." I tried to explain it the way my mother told it to me. But even while I explained it to Pete I still didn't really see why I should have to give up my fun just because my folks couldn't stand each other. It sure did stink. But I didn't want to tell Pete that. No guy likes to talk bad about his folks, even to his friends.

We were walking down the main street leading to the long block of stores which lined both sides of the street.

"Where you gonna look first?" Pete asked.

"Jeez, I don't know." I started thinking about the different jobs I would try for.

There was another major street which crossed over the shopping center that also had stores. I thought about that street and figured that the only places where I would ever want a job would be in the luncheonette or the hardware store. The other stores were mostly ladies' stuff and there was just no way I would be caught working in places like that. But then there was the sporting goods store . . .

"Hey, Scott," Pete interrupted my thinking, "what if you can't get a job?"

Jeez, wasn't that just like Pete. He never let up when he wanted something. He really wasn't happy about me working. That was for sure.

"Get off my back, will you?" I gave him a soft sock on the arm and started to cross over. Jeez, I was scared. I knew inside that there might not be any jobs. Besides, it was awful tough asking people for a job . . .

"Well, where're you gonna go first?" Pete asked.

The street was crowded with shoppers and lookers. I saw a lot of guys I knew. *Boy, it would be great if I didn't have to get a job and could just hang around like usual,* I thought to myself.

"Well?" Pete asked. "How about the depart-

and make people walking together split up if they want to get past. That action always gave me a kick, making people do what I wanted. Pete looked at me and we both broke up. We always did that too, when it worked.

"Come on, Scott, get finished with this job-hunting stuff so we can still have time to ride up to the reservoir this afternoon."

"Aw, I don't know if I want to go up there today. I still have to get a job or my old lady will be on my back." I remembered what my mother had said about needing help and all, but then I thought about how great it would be to get on my bike and ride up to the reservoir. There weren't going to be too many more good days left before the weather turned winter cold. "Is anybody gonna be there today?"

"A couple of the guys are goin' and so are some girls."

"No kiddin'? How about big tits, is she gonna be there?" That always got to Pete. He was still kind of funny about girls and sex and stuff so I loved to bug him about it.

"I don't know, but I want to go. Are you gonna go or not? I don't want to kill the whole day just standing around waiting for you if you're not gonna go up there with me later."

I could tell he was getting sore at me. He didn't have much success with girls. I didn't know why. But I figured maybe he came on too strong and scared them away. Or maybe he was scared of them and acted repulsive so they would turn him down. Anyway, they sure gave him a hard time.

"Aw, take it easy, Pete. I didn't say I wouldn't go with you." I was thinking that I really didn't want to go job hunting by myself. Pete could bug me but I liked having him around. He was one smart guy and the only one of the guys I could really talk with about important, serious things . . . "Okay, wait a sec for me. I'll just run in this one store and see if they have anything for me. Then we can go get our bikes."

I figured I could try the other places some other time. After all, what was the hurry, I thought. I had plenty of time. Pete took hold of my arm.

"What would you do in a store like this?" he said, pointing to the sign above the store window. LIVING LEATHER, it read.

The place made handcrafted leather goods. It was something I really wanted to learn how to do. I had thought about it ever since I found out how great it was to make stuff I could really use, like the belt I made in camp last year. It was better than any of the store-bought ones I ever had. I thought if I worked in a store like that I could get to learn more about it. Maybe I'd even go into business for myself one day.

"Some guy in camp last summer told me about this place," I told Pete. "He was our arts and crafts counselor. You should've seen the terrific sandals and belts he made. He even made vests. He sold the stuff he made and was really piling in the dough."

Pete didn't look too impressed so I figured I wouldn't go on. Instead I shook his hand off my arm and went into the store.

I looked around the walls of the store and saw all the bags and belts hanging up. I wondered how much it would cost to buy enough leather to get a business started.

"Hey, man, we really would like to help you out and all but there just isn't enough business around here to hire anybody at all." The blond, bearded man with the long hair turned toward the other guy with the Afro hairdo who was sitting at a machine sewing on some red-brown leather. "We barely make it ourselves. That's right, Art, isn't it?"

"That's the way it is, fella. Business just isn't too good right now," the guy named Art said, nodding his head at his partner. They looked kind of sad, the two of them. I figured that maybe things weren't so great in the leather business after all. But I figured that I ought to say something else to them.

"Well, listen, if things get better and you ever need somebody to help, would you call me?" I looked around me and smelled the leather. It smelled awful good, clean and sharp. I wrote my name and telephone number on a small piece of paper and gave it to the blond guy. I could see they were telling me the truth. The place didn't seem to have much going on.

Like there were no customers in the place. So I told them good-bye and thanked them for talking with me. You never know, I figured, just how things might turn out. Besides it really seemed to be the kind of work I could get turned on to. I walked out the front door knowing deep inside that I wasn't ever going to hear from those guys. They'd probably go out of business the way it looked to me. *Jeez, that's just like it,* I thought, getting mad, *just when I find something really great I'd like to do . . . My lousy luck . . .*

"Well?" Pete stood there in front of me as I walked out the door.

"Well, nothing." I felt rotten, too sick to talk about it. *There's no use trying to get a job,* I thought. *Anything good will probably be taken.* "The hell with it, Pete," I said, smacking him hard on his shoulder, making him wince with pain. "Let's get our bikes and go to the reservoir."

"Okay, man," Pete said, grinning happily while rubbing his shoulder, "now you're getting smart."

But Dave, there just aren't any jobs," I insisted. The two of us were up in the bedroom doing our homework after dinner. It had ended up a swell day. Pete and I really had a ball with everyone at the reservoir. One of the guys had his car up there and we all took turns riding on the hood while he drove us around. I slipped off and almost broke my ass. Jeez, did it hurt riding my bike back home.

"Ma is right," Dave said. "You didn't try enough places."

"Like hell! What do you know? Just 'cause you have a job . . ."

"That's not the point."

"Aw, what's the use, there just aren't any

jobs for a guy my age. So why bust my balls?" I slammed shut the book that lay on the desk in front of me. *Who the hell wants to do homework when everything stinks?* I got up and left the room. I went downstairs to the kitchen.

"What are you doing here, Scott? You should be doing your homework."

My mother looked up from the kitchen table where she had her checkbook lying open in front of her. The whole table was a mess with checks and bills and papers all over the place. *Jeez,* I thought, *if I ever let my desk look like that she'd murder me.* I was going to say something about it but then I noticed she really looked dragged out. There were lines on her face I never saw there before. It gave me a funny feeling.

"I just thought I'd take a break, that's all."

"But you just went upstairs less than ten minutes ago."

I went over to the cabinet above the sink and got out a cup.

"Scott, please don't make a mess," she said. "I'm trying to get our bills cleaned up and I don't want to have to bother with you at the same time."

"Don't worry, I'm just gonna get a drink."

"Yes, but your drink usually ends up with a mess all over everything. I don't want to have to clean up the kitchen again tonight." Her voice sounded like she would start screaming at me any second.

"Don't worry," I told her again. *She gets*

hysterical about everything lately, I thought. I was sore at her nagging at me all the time. It was always for the same thing, too. It was like I was the only person in the house who ever dirtied anything. I wasn't. But I sure was the only one who ever got hollered at.

I boiled some water and filled my cup, stirring in the tiny spots of coffee and watching them dissolve and turn the water dark.

"No kiddin', ma, what am I gonna do for some money?" I hoped she knew the answer because I couldn't figure anything out.

"Not now, Scott. Can't you see I'm adding?"

I carried my cup to the table, trying not to spill any of the coffee on the floor.

"Don't make yourself too comfortable, Scott," my mother said as she wrote something at the bottom of a column of figures.

"Aw, ma . . ."

"I mean it, you have to do your homework, and especially your algebra."

She was still sore at me because Mr. Schmidt wrote her a note about my not bringing in my homework on the day after dad left us. She couldn't seem to understand what dad's leaving had to do with my not doing my homework. *She acts like a real nerd sometimes,* I thought, watching her write out a check to somebody.

I sipped my hot coffee carefully. I didn't want to go back up to the room, and I didn't want to stay there with my mother in such a lousy mood. I didn't know what I wanted. I was all mixed up lately. Everybody was on my back. They all stank. The whole world stank. Nobody gave a damn for me, especially my folks.

"You know, you and dad are supposed to take care of me. I don't really have to get a job if I don't want," I burst out, really pissed off at all her nagging at me. After all, Pete told me what the law was. So why should I have to knock myself out? They were supposed to be doing that, not me.

"We're responsible for you," she said, looking at me real hard. "We do take care of you. But you have to do something, too." Her voice was low and each word came out cold and clean, hitting me like punches. The look on her face made me shut up. She looked mad enough to kill me. I was scared. That wasn't like her. She was never into the strong-arm stuff like some parents. But right then I bet if she had a bat in her hand she would've hit me with it, hard. Instead she just sat there looking at me like I was somebody she never saw before. Finally she just shook her head at me and went back to work.

I drank the rest of my coffee without talking. The work she was doing sure looked boring. She didn't seem to like doing it any more than I liked doing my homework. After a while I didn't feel like staying there watching her. It was no fun seeing how tired and worried she looked. I was starting to feel like a louse for hollering at her about my troubles. So I put my empty cup in the sink and went back up to my room.

Dave was still busy writing away. Dave never seemed to have any problems. Everything was always so easy for him. He got good marks in school. He got a job with no sweat. At that moment, I wanted to go over and sock him.

"Ma really stinks."

"Shut up Scott, and do your homework."

"Boy, you're beginning to sound like ma."

Dave looked up at me then. And he didn't look too pleased with me.

"Jeez, Dave, if it weren't for her I wouldn't be in this fix. Just because she and dad are jerks we have to suffer."

"Do your homework," Dave answered, as he went back to his writing.

I left and went into my mother's room. The extension phone was there. I closed the door tightly and dialed Pete's number.

"Pete, is that you?" I asked the answering voice on the phone.

"Of course it's me."

It was a stupid question because Pete had his own personal phone. He even had his name listed in the telephone book. Boy, he had it all. His parents were really great to him . . .

"What's up?" Pete asked.

"The same old crap," I told him. "There's just no way for me to get any money around here."

"Did you talk to your mother like I told you?"

"Aw, she couldn't care less. Y'know I can't

even get enough money to go to a movie with you guys. I don't know what to do now." I was glad that the phone was between us because I really felt like crying and I guessed if Pete saw my face he would know.

"How about your old man; do you think if you asked him he'd come across?"

"Naw, Dave talked with him a long time ago and my dad told him there just was no way for him to give us an allowance. He told Dave we'd have to find a way to earn our own money. That was great for Dave, he got a job with no sweat. But you know I've tried and there's just nothing around here for me."

"Boy, your parents sure are rough on you," Pete said.

"Yeah, it really stinks around here lately," I told him. Except for Pete no one cared about what happened to me. Dave and my mother were at me if I even opened my mouth. They wouldn't even try to understand how tough it was for me. I bet my mother hated me. She sure acted like it. Pete was the only person who gave a damn or bothered to listen to me. I was going to tell him that when I heard something click in my ear.

"Hey, what's that?" I asked Pete, wondering if he heard the same sound.

Before Pete could answer my mother's voice sounded in my ear. "It's Mother, Scott. I want to make a phone call."

"I just got on the phone," I told her.

"You aren't supposed to be on the phone at all! So please get off right now and go do your homework."

I could have killed her for talking like that with Pete listening on the other end of the line. She was getting worse every day. No wonder my dad was so pissed with her, I thought, feeling scared at how mad I was at her.

"Well, I'm waiting," she nagged.

"Just two seconds. I'll get off in just two seconds, okay?"

The click on the receiver told me she agreed and had hung up the extension phone downstairs.

"Wow, you really got it hard!" Pete said, making me feel even worse somehow.

I wanted to tell him what I thought about her but I just couldn't get myself to do it.

"Aw, she's all right, I guess. She's just upset about the bills and my old man and everything, that's all." It was funny because when I said that to Pete I almost believed it myself. But it just didn't seem right somehow that she was always bugging me, not Dave or Lisa, only me. Maybe she really did hate me. I didn't want to say she was a rotten mother to Pete but she sure was acting different to me now that dad wasn't around. I swallowed the hard rock that seemed to be stuck in my throat.

"Well," I managed to croak out to Pete, "I'll

pick you up at the usual time tomorrow, okay?"

"Yeah, sure . . . but Scott, am I glad that I don't have to live in your house . . ."

"Yeah, well . . . I'll see you in the morning." I hung up the phone hard. I wanted to break something that was hers.

I was just lying on her bed, staring at the lights coming off the chandelier on the ceiling and thinking about how it used to be before my dad left us when the door to the room opened and she stood there in the doorway looking down at me.

I was feeling pretty bad already but seeing her standing there like that made me feel even worse.

She looked the same, but something had changed. She just didn't look like she used to, like before my father left. Nothing was like it used to be.

"This is not doing your homework, Scott," she said.

"Goddamn, ma, what'd you do that for?" I asked.

"What did I do what for?"

"Talk on the phone like that."

"Look, Scott, I have a job to do and so do you. Your job tonight is doing your homework, not talking on the phone to Pete all night."

"But I just got on the phone . . ." I started to explain.

"And please take your filthy shoes off my bed!"

"That's what's wrong. You always do that." I had started to shout because I had to make her listen to me.

"That's enough! You're just wasting time. Now go and do your homework. This is not the time for a discussion."

"Sure, what do you care about me and my problems . . ." I was feeling sick inside. My stomach felt like it had turned green or something. My throat ached.

"Scott, get off my bed now!"

I pulled myself off the bed and walked across the room till I stood right in front of her. I was half a head taller than her, but lately I had begun to feel like I was a little kid again. Sometimes when no one would listen to me I began to think maybe I was invisible or something. Maybe that's what they wanted me to be, because that's how everybody was treating me.

"All right, go on and get back to your homework." She left the doorway and stepped around me, leaving an empty hallway in front of me. I looked at the closed door to my room on the right-hand wall of the hallway. *What's the point*, I thought to myself, *nothing I do will make her like me.*

But I turned around anyway and watched her sit down on the edge of her bed.

"Ma," I began. I didn't know what I wanted to say to her. That was the problem. I wanted to talk to her. I wanted her to talk with me, listen to me, like me the way she used to. My stomach was grinding and I felt a cutting pain like I was getting the runs, like real bad cramps.

Something happened then, because my mother looked at my face and suddenly she said to me, "All right, Scott, tell me *fast*." But her words came out like a sigh. She had taken off her shoes and was rubbing the bottoms of her feet. Jeez, she looked beat. I began to feel sorry for her . . .

"It's the job. I tried, no kidding, really." I talked fast, trying to convince her. "There just aren't any jobs around."

She started to answer me, but I didn't give her the chance.

"It's just not fair. I can't even go to a movie or get a soda with the guys." My words had begun to come out too quick and I could feel tears coming into my throat. I didn't want to cry. I just wanted to make her understand. A guy just couldn't go around without some money in his pocket. Everybody would think he was weird or something.

"Besides," I said, hurrying on, "I have things to buy for school and I'll get in trouble if I can't get them." She seemed to be listening. Maybe, I thought, she understood after all.

"Scott, I understand . . ." she started to say.

"No, you don't! How could you?" I shouted back quickly, not wanting to listen to her.

She pulled herself onto the bed so that her back was resting on the headboard and her feet were stretched out in front of her. Her hand reached over to the night table and she pulled off a book that was there. She opened it up to where there was a bookmark. She fingered the edge of the page for a minute still looking at me. The she looked down at the page in her lap like she had decided to read the book. She didn't give a damn about me. I was right. She'd rather read her rotten book than listen to me. Just when I decided that there was no point in my standing there anymore, she looked up at me.

"Scott, I'm awfully tired." Her voice was very low, like she was almost asleep. "I've been working all day at a job I hate. I came home this evening hoping to get some rest and instead I found that I had to work over the bills. You kids never even thought to lift a finger to help with dinner or the dishes . . ."

"Aw, ma." I didn't want to talk about dishes . . . She always managed to do that, change the subject like that. Since she got a job she was always giving me the business about how if she could go get a job when she never worked before so could I. Or, if I really wanted something bad enough, I'd find a way. And now she was talking about dishes.

"Why are you always picking on me? What about Dave and Lisa? They make dishes, too!" I was tired of getting blamed for everything. She never picked on anybody else.

"Oh God, I'm tired of all of you. No one around here ever makes any dishes, but the sink is always full every time I look in the kitchen.

Maybe some strangers have a key to the house and sneak in here when we aren't in and eat our food and leave their mess all over the house?"

Her voice had gotten louder and she looked like she was going to explode any second. I wanted to calm her down because the way I felt I didn't want to make a federal case out of it, not when I was trying to get her to agree that I should be getting some money from either her or dad. But I never did get the chance because right in the middle of her hollering she stopped dead, took a deep breath, and said with her voice back to normal, "All right, Scott, enough is enough. You have to get back to your homework or you'll be up all night again trying to get it done."

It happened again. Just like always. I tried to talk seriously with her and she just turned me off.

"You're something else," I heard myself screaming at her. "You don't give a damn about me. What the hell, you've got all the money you need. You can buy anything you want . . ."

Her hand came up signaling me to stop. But I couldn't, not anymore.

"You hate dad so you have to take it out on me. You think I'm like him, that's why you hate me . . ."

"Scott . . ." she tried to stop me again. Even though this time she sat straight up on the bed and glared at me, I had to go on.

"You have to take care of me. Dad gives you

money for us and that money is ours. You have to give me some kind of an allowance. Why should Lisa have it so easy just 'cause she's younger than me?" The words came out fast. I really didn't hear what I was saying anymore but I could see the look of anger on my mother's face telling me I had gone too far.

"That's enough," she shouted back at me, making my mouth stop flapping. "You lazy, spoiled brat. Who do you think you are? No one owes you anything. You're old enough to earn your keep and if you won't do it then you just can't put out your hand to me. How dare you tell me how to spend the money I get for you from your father? If you don't like the way it is here with me, then pack up your things and go find someplace else."

Her words came out at me like bullets, fast and hard. They smacked into my brain and made my head hurt. I wanted to run out of the room, but instead I stood there, my feet stuck on the floor, her words hammering at me, making me feel smaller and smaller. I concentrated on making the floor open up and swallow me, but nothing much happened. Finally I couldn't take the pain anymore.

"I don't have to live here. I can live at Pete's. He's got parents who love him. They wouldn't do to him what you and dad did to us. You hate me and wish I was dead, don't you?" I had screamed out the words so loud that the silence scared me when I stopped shouting. My throat was dry like I had been running around the track at school.

"Oh my God!" she said, putting her hands over her face so that her words came out kind of muffled. I thought for a second maybe she was crying or something. There was a sharp stab of pain in my head like a knife was suddenly stuck into me. I couldn't see her face and her shoulders were all hunched over. I wanted to say something so that I would know if she was all right. I wanted to move toward her, to touch her and see her face again. I couldn't move.

After a long time she finally rubbed her face with her hands and looked up at me. Her eyes looked awful full. I swallowed hard, feeling like a rat for making her look like that.

"Scott, I love you. I love your brother and sister too, with all my heart and soul. If it weren't for you kids . . ." Her voice kind of faded away. Then after a second she started again.

"How can I make you understand what has been happening to me . . ."

I felt the muscles in my body begin to relax. I began to think . . . to hope . . .

She sat quiet like she was thinking. There was a faraway look on her face. But just when I figured maybe I had finally reached her . . .

"Scott, we just can't start having this kind of discussion when I'm exhausted and can't think straight. Besides, you're really only delaying

doing your homework." I had been right all the
time. Her words were like a quick dive into an
icy pool. I was back down in the real world
again. There wasn't any other.

I knew for sure now that there wasn't any
use trying to get her to understand. It never
would be any use. Nothing really mattered much
anymore.

She put her back up against the headboard
again and started to read the book in her lap. She
didn't look up again. She was finished. It was
over. I hated her! I turned and left her room,
never wanting to talk to her or see her again. I
only wanted to get away. Go someplace where
someone would care, would understand how a
person felt.

I got back into my room and found Dave in
the same position I had left my mother. *He's just
like her,* I thought, hating him, too.

"Dave?"

"Yeah?" he mumbled and didn't look up
from his book.

"What's happening around here? I can't talk
to anybody. Ma's different. She doesn't ever
have time to talk with me . . ."

"Ma's got a lot on her mind, that's all," Dave
said.

"I know that. But what I don't get is why she
can't at least try to understand. I tried to get a
job, but there just aren't any around. Everything's gone."

"Some try, two places. If you really wanted a job I could probably get you one washing dishes at the place where I work . . ."

"What kinda job is that?" I said, thinking about how crummy washing dishes, even for money, would be.

"That's just what we're telling you. You really don't want a job, because if you did you could get one. So why don't you shut up and stop complaining for a change." He started to go back to his reading.

I ran over to his bed and rammed my fist into his belly as hard as I could. I wanted to hurt him, hurt someone.

He was a big guy. He outreached me by half a foot. He could have murdered me any time he really wanted. But somehow he always stopped short of doing any bad stuff to me. He grabbed me down onto his bed and punched me hard a couple of times, holding me down with the weight of his body. His knees tied my arms tight to my sides. He was strong, man. His fist smacked into me and I could feel the pain shoot up my shoulder into the back of my head. He must have figured that he had given me enough because he loosened his grip then and gave me a chance to free my arms. I got a good shot on him right into his chest. If it had been anyone else he would have hollered in pain, but not Dave. He grabbed me again, tight, wrapping his arms and legs around me like a boa constrictor. He squeezed me till I had no breath left in my lungs. Jeez, I felt like I was dying.

"Have you had it?" he hissed into my ear.

It took all my remaining breath and strength to whisper a small no. I wouldn't stop. I wanted to hit. I wanted to fight. I wanted to shut out all my mother had said to me. I wanted somebody to touch, hear, and see me. It didn't matter how I got it to happen, but it had to. I could feel the tears coming.

"Okay, now stop crapping around," Dave warned.

He began to release the tension of his body muscles and started to unwind his legs and arms from around me.

"Just cut it out or I'll break you in two. You understand?" But his voice wasn't mad or anything. He had to say that I supposed. Just like I had to answer him with another sock from my freed hand.

He knew I was beaten but he let me play it like I was only tired. That's how it was with us. We never talked about it, but Dave understood. Dave knew about how a guy felt when he got beaten. He didn't rub it in this time either.

"Hey, screwball, get off my back and let me get some work done, will you?" he asked as I left his bedside, rubbing my sore arm.

"Yeah . . . I know . . . everybody's busy." Inside I told myself there wasn't any point trying to talk to anybody in the house anymore. I'd had it with them all, especially with my mother. She didn't give a damn about me no matter what she said. Why should I bother to try any more, it didn't matter to anybody what I did so long as I didn't bother them.

I sat down at my desk and tried to concentrate on my homework, but it all looked like so much jibberish. I had a bigger problem on my mind. It was bigger than just getting money. I had to find some place to go, to get away from this house. I didn't know where I could go, but I had to get away. My dad had no room for me to stay with him. Probably he wouldn't want me around any more than my mother did.

I sat for a long time staring at the wall in front of my desk. Sometimes if I concentrated on drawing something special, ideas would pop into my head. But tonight I didn't even want to try. I knew nothing would work for me. There didn't seem to be any answers I could find that told me what would happen to me. I only knew since my dad left it had all been bad. I wasn't going to stick around for more of the same. I had to find somewhere else to live, and soon.

Scott, get your ass in here and get this kitchen cleaned up." Dave's voice rose over the sound coming out of the TV.

"Jeez, Dave," I shouted back, sore because he was making me miss the most important part of the program, "I'll do it in a minute."

"Yeah, that's what you said yesterday." He had come into the den and was standing in front of me so I couldn't even watch the action on the tube.

"Goddamn, Dave, get the hell out of the way." I shoved my fist into his belly. But he was far enough away so that I lost my balance and fell off my seat on the sofa and went down onto the floor.

"Okay, come on and get busy," Dave said, grabbing a handful of my hair and pulling me to my feet. "Ma will be home any minute now and I don't want to get blamed because of your mess."

"Ma won't be home for hours," I said, trying to pull away from him. He had moved his hand from my hair to a tight grip on my arm.

Since my mother had started working at a second job weekends and evenings selling real estate, Dave had taken over the house like he was the father. He'd boss Lisa and me worse than our mother ever did. I had thought with my mother away so much things would get better. But no way. Dave acted like he was Mr. Big Shit.

"Dave," I pleaded, "I just want to finish watching this show, then I'll do the dishes."

Dave's grip on my arm didn't loosen. He started dragging me toward the kitchen doorway. I tried winding my foot around the back of his leg so I could throw him down on the floor but instead we both went down, with his 160 pounds of pure pointed bones digging into my body when he landed on top of me.

"Jeez, Dave get the hell offa me and let me alone." I forced out the words as I tried to squeeze out from under his body.

We rolled around a couple of times on the den floor with me getting the worst of it. After a while I figured Dave got tired of acting like an asshole and he let me up.

I looked at the television and saw my program was over. That really made me sore.

"Dammit, Dave, look what you did. You made me miss the best part of the story." I felt like socking him but I didn't want to start that stuff all over again. I still ached in the places where his elbows and knees landed during the last round.

"Stop crapping around, Scott, and get the kitchen clean."

"Jeez, Dave, you have a one track mind," I said, hating him for being so big that I couldn't beat him up. "I didn't make all those dishes. You ate too."

"Scott, I'm going to break your ass if you don't get in there and do those dishes. When ma came home last night and saw that sink full I got blamed. I'm not going to let that happen again."

He looked at me with murder in his eyes, so I decided I might as well get it over with and do the dishes. But not before I got a good dig into his back as I walked around him into the kitchen.

He let that one go by, but I knew later on he'd try to get even. Dave was turning out to be an A-number-1 louse. The more my mother was away the meaner he got. It was like he hated Lisa and me because he was stuck with the job of watching out for us.

What griped me about Dave was his treating us like he had to really take care of us. I was no baby, neither was Lisa. Dave acted like he was stuck with a couple of three-year-olds. He never talked to me like he used to and he sure never listened to anything I had to say. The only time he opened his mouth now was to boss me around.

Boy, am I glad Pete's house is just around the corner, I thought as I shoved the dishes into the machine. I ate most of my meals there so I could get away from Dave and ma some of the time. *I don't know how much more I can take of this shit*, I thought as I scrapped the leftover gunk off the dishes into the garbage bag.

The phone rang just then.

"Hey, Dave," I hollered, "get it, will you? My hands are all wet." If I didn't tell him to answer the phone he'd just let it ring. That really drove me up a wall. Lisa always had her bedroom door shut tight and never heard anything. Neither one of them ever wanted to answer the phone because it was usually a call for me. But this time Dave broke his heart and answered the phone. I knew I should have known better than to let him do me a favor.

"He's busy doing the dishes now . . . Okay, yeah . . . good-bye." I hollered to Dave not to hang up because I was wiping my hands dry. But not him. He got deaf whenever I said anything.

"Dammit, Dave, why'd you do that?" I shouted at him. I was mad. It was too much. Now he was starting to boss around my friends, too.

"It was just Pete," Dave said, just like that. Like, what the heck, Pete was just a nobody. *Sure,* I thought, burning inside, *if it was somebody for him . . .*

"I've had it, man," I screamed at him, throwing the towel down on the table. "I'm getting out of this house and away from you and ma for good."

I didn't bother to take anything but my comb and toothbrush with me. I moved into Pete's house that night before my mother got back from work. I bet Dave was glad to see me go, because he didn't make a move to stop me.

Pete didn't even bother asking his parents if I could stay there. We figured they had so many kids hanging around the house all the time they wouldn't even notice my moving in. We were right. Maybe it was because I had eaten so many meals over there lately they just got used to having me around. In any case they didn't make out like they noticed any difference.

It was funny about Pete's parents. They were around a lot but it was like they weren't. I couldn't figure out why it felt that way. I did think it was pretty weird when nobody said anything about my moving in. It was like going to a hotel except Pete's folks didn't ask for money. Nobody really cared what anybody was doing or where they were or anything. It was really great after all the crap and stuff I'd been taking at home with Dave and ma.

Pete had his own room, too. It was a great

room, kind of off in a quiet corner where nobody ever bothered us. It was a big house with lots of staircases leading off into different parts of the house. Pete's room was at the end of the stairs coming out of the kitchen. Pete told me it must have been a maid's room once because it was separated from the other bedrooms in the house. We could play records all night and no one could hear us. It was great.

Every once in a while I'd run around the corner to my house to get some clean clothes. First, though, I'd call up to make sure Dave or my mother weren't home.

Especially my mother.

I didn't want to start in with her.

When I'd go back to the house I'd get some clean stuff out of my bureau drawers, then I'd leave a note on the kitchen table and my dirty clothes in the wash basket. That was just to let them know I was okay. I knew they were just as happy I was gone and not around to bother them anymore because nobody ever called Pete's to find out if I was still alive.

"Hey, Scott, you know what?" Pete's face looked full of a good idea. Pete had a face I could read. It always told what was on his mind. I could see he was really buzzing with something. He was that turned on.

"What?"

"My folks are gonna be away this weekend."

I had been at Pete's almost two weeks and in all that time I couldn't really say that his folks were ever around. I mean, they were there in the house all right. But they weren't around. Like they didn't pay any attention to what we were doing. His folks never asked Pete if he did his homework or where he was going or what the money he wanted was for. Things like that. So now I couldn't understand what Pete was getting all excited about.

"So what's the big deal?" I asked.

"We can throw a party, that's what."

And we did. It was the wildest, craziest night I ever spent. But it wasn't just the party that made it that way.

Pete and I hollered good-bye as the last guy and his girlfriend left the party. It was really late. I mean it was really early. Like it was six o'clock in the morning. Boy, I was exhausted.

"Holy Christ, Scott," Pete said with a heavy sort of whispered sigh. His eyes were wide open. "Look at this mess."

I looked around the room and saw what he meant. It had been quite a party. Pete had acted like a real nitwit. When he had let the guys get way out of hand I had thought about trying to stop them, but by that time they were too far gone to control. Besides, Pete was doing his best to egg everyone on and I wasn't about to cross him when he was acting like he was out of his head. A guy could get killed trying to be a hero. That was a lesson I had learned when I was a little kid in grade school.

I had tried to save some new kid in my class from a bunch of guys having a spitting contest with him as the target. That poor little kid was covered all over with the stuff. The guys had surrounded him and he couldn't do anything but stand there crying and trying to cover his face. I was only a little kid myself, like nine or ten, but I couldn't just stand there and watch. So I tried to break up the party and they ended up spitting on me. I was just as bad off as the kid I was trying to rescue. The principal and my mother thought I was just great. But I learned my lesson that day. I was no hero and didn't care who knew it.

"Hey, I'm too beat to start cleaning up now. Let's go to bed. We can clean up tomorrow," Pete said, yawning his head off.

"Whatdya mean?" I said, knowing damn well what he meant. "I'm not gonna clean up this mess all alone with you." I walked around the room as I talked. There wasn't a clean spot anywhere I could see. I was disgusted. "It's not my fault you let the guys go crazy," I said. I looked over to where some vomit decorated an oriental carpet.

Wow, I thought, as my stomach turned over, *I'd get killed if that ever happened in my house.*

"How'd I know that Ted's girlfriend couldn't hold her booze?"

"Jeez, Pete, you know damn well that pot and booze don't mix. And all that popcorn, too. Yech," I said, disgusted with the whole mess.

I was really getting nauseous from the sight and smells around us. The mess wasn't in just one room either. The party had grown too big to keep in just one room. There must have been around fifty or sixty people spread throughout the house, coming and going all night. Pete should have figured out that was going to happen. We lived in a town where word goes out awful fast if someone is giving a party. Especially someone like Pete, who everybody knew gets bombed out of his mind and wouldn't give a damn about what went on.

"Come on," I said. I was dead on my feet, besides feeling queazier than hell. There was no point in fighting with Pete when I felt so lousy. "Let's get some sleep and we'll call up some of the guys in the morning to help us get rid of this mess."

Pete was on the down end of a high and looked really zonked out. It was funny about Pete. He seemed like an awful smart guy in some ways but he sure could act like a jack-ass.

"You really ought to lay off the grass, Pete. It blows your mind too much." I knew I should've kept my face shut on that subject. Pete really got pissed off whenever I said anything about it. But it bugged the hell out of me to watch Pete mess himself up. He seemed to lose all his self-control when he got high and really started acting crazy wild. It was nuts because he was high most of the time without needing any extra help. *Jeez, who knows what it's doing to his brains,* I thought.

That stuff really scared me. Once I saw a guy freak out on just a couple of drags. He just went into convulsions and we had to call a doctor to quiet him down. What really blew my mind was watching him all out of control, throwing his body around the room like a lunatic—his arms and legs all rigid sometimes, then all loose and wild, like they had no bones in them, flaying around like a shaking rag doll. We never did find out whether it was the pot that was the cause, but I wasn't going to take any chances.

"Listen, you chicken fink," Pete hissed at me real slow and low, "just 'cause you're scared yellow don't think you're so great." He stopped then, like he lost his thoughts for a minute. The mean expression on his face changed suddenly and a cockeyed grin came over it. His eyebrows were raised and his eyes seemed to sparkle. "Anyhow, Scott, you don't know how great this feeling is," he said. While he talked he kind of rocked back and forth on the balls of his feet.

Now, I was a beer drinker, myself. And even though it was only a mild brew, I could get a glow going on it. It was a great feeling. Pete was right about that, there's nothing quite like a really good high. But at least even when I was high I knew what I was doing and when to stop, which was more than I could say for Pete.

"Watch out," I shouted. But it was too late. Pete had tripped on the third step on our way up to his room. He must have been having a tough time lifting up his feet because his toe seemed to have gotten caught under the lip of the next step and down he went. He whacked his forehead on the edge of a step. I could hear the crack as his knees landed on the floor below. I had tried to make a grab for him but it all happened too fast.

"You okay?" I asked, figuring that he must've knocked himself out. But not Pete. He sat back on the floor, looked up at me with his silly grin, and started to giggle. I could see the red welt on his forehead starting to swell. But Pete didn't seem to be feeling any pain. *He will really feel it tomorrow*, I thought. Then it hit me.

"Hey, Pete, when are your folks coming back here?"

"Aw, I don't know. Tomorrow, I guess," a groggy Pete answered.

"Pete, man," I said, beginning to feel frantic, "this is tomorrow."

"Let's get some sleep." Pete was too far gone to pay any attention to me. He got up heavily and began to take the steps, slowly this time and carefully. He'd lift his foot real high, then let it drop down on the next step. Then he'd think a while before he'd try the other foot. It must have been fifteen minutes before we finally got up to his room.

Neither one of us got undressed. Any worry I had about the mess downstairs I forgot about fast. After all, Pete's parents wouldn't care about stuff like that. Pete didn't act worried, so I figured it would be stupid for me to get upset about it. *What the hell,* I thought, *maybe tomorrow isn't today after all.* The world went blank once my head hit the pillow.

I was kind of half awake when I heard the noise. It was a muffled sound. First I heard a high, shrieky tone and then I heard what sounded like a low rumbling. I lay there on the bed and tried to make out just where the noise was coming from. Pete's bedroom door was closed so I knew the only possible place where the sound could come from was the kitchen. My head was aching so hard I didn't want to think about anything but just rolling over and getting back to sleep. I glanced over at Pete's bed. All I could see was a long mountain of blanket and a white pillow which had a mess of dark hair in the middle of it.

He's still dead to the world, I thought,

yawning. I started to roll over on my belly, burying my arms and head into my pillow. *Boy, am I beat; it's gonna be great just to sleep the whole day away.*

"Pete," a man's voice followed the pounding on the bedroom door.

"Hey, Pete," I whispered as I jumped up out of my bed still dazed and kind of dizzy from not enough sleep. "Pete, wake up." I grabbed a part of the blanket I figured must be covering his shoulder and gave a push.

"Don't bother me," came the muffled answer from under the blanket.

"Pete," but I didn't have time to say anything more. The bedroom door opened up wide and there was Pete's father standing in the doorway. He looked burned up. I wanted to disappear, fast.

"What the hell has happened in this house?"

I wasn't going to say a word. I just stood there, to one side of the room, hoping his father wouldn't look at me.

"I want to see you both downstairs in two minutes. That's an order. You hear me?" By this time even Pete was sitting up in his bed. We both just nodded our heads.

Pete's father turned and went back down the stairs, throwing back a last-minute order over his shoulder at us, "Move your asses and fast!"

"It's not my fault you've spoiled the kid rotten." I looked at Pete's face as we came down into the kitchen just as Pete's father was in the middle of hollering at Pete's mother. I was glad Pete's uncombed hair was long enough to hide the swollen bruise on his forehead. *We look bad enough,* I thought, scared his father would have something else to holler about.

The way he was yelling at Pete's mother made me feel lousy. Pete's dad was really giving her hell. I hated being there, listening. It was just like when my father yelled at my mother. I looked at Pete, hoping he would say something and get his father off his mother's back.

Suddenly Pete's mother screamed out, "You damned beast." She didn't looked scared at all. "You're the one that wanted all these damn kids in the first place. You and your giant male ego."

I was sweating. Pete looked like he was dead. He had gone all white and still. I would have grabbed his arm and pulled him back upstairs but it was too late.

"And you rotten kids." His mother turned toward us. "What the hell were you doing here last night?"

The two of us just stood there, trapped and afraid to say anything.

"Pete," his father said, "answer your mother."

Pete looked at me like he was begging me to save him or something.

"We had a little party." I said it very low and kept my head down so that all I could see was the tops of my hiking boots. I let my mind wander around remembering stuff so I didn't have to think about what Pete's folks were saying to us and especially to Pete.

They really hated Pete. The way they beat down on him that day I figured they must've hated him for a long time, too. They must've said they were sorry he was born ten times a minute. They called him an awful lot of rotten names, too. His mother really laid it on him with language I couldn't believe. It blew my mind to hear that tiny lady screaming like that. And what she didn't call Pete, his father did. They ripped him into little bleeding pieces.

I was hurting bad for him but there wasn't anything I could do to help. I was just glad they weren't screaming at me.

"Those damned brats drank up all the Scotch," Pete's mother shrieked.

"Good for them. It'll mean less for you." Pete's dad was kind of leering at her. "Maybe you'll be able to see straight enough to make dinner for a change." Pete's father looked like he wanted to punch her one in the mouth. I felt just as scared as when my parents used to fight. I listened to them taking pot shots at each other. In between their shouting and screaming at each other they batted out some orders to Pete and me.

"And you better get this house cleaned up, fast." His father said, finally giving the two of us a chance to agree with him enthusiastically so we could beat it the hell out of the room.

One line Pete's mother hollered at me really blew my mind. As we were leaving the room she yelled after me, "I'm going to tell your mother what a disgusting and irresponsible slob you are the next time she calls to find out about her dear little boy!"

Her words flashed a light on in my mind. I turned and asked her, "What do you mean? When does my mother ever call here?"

"Every damn day since you arrived, Mr. Smart Face," she shouted back at me.

My mother calls every day. How about that? I felt like I just sucked on a lemon only to find out it was filled with the sweetest-tasting syrup ever. But that feeling didn't have a chance to last too long. It lasted as long as it took to get from the kitchen to the horrible mess we had to clean up.

"Jeez," I whispered loudly to Pete, "no wonder your folks are sore. This place looks even worse than it did last night."

We had both been too whacked out the night before to really take it all in.

Chairs were overturned. There were spilled drinks on the floors and tables. Cigarette ashes filled the ashtrays and covered most of the floor and carpeting. Butts were everywhere and so were peanut shells, popcorn, and pretzels. A lot of them were mashed up and mixed into the puddles of spilled drinks. Stamped-on pieces of pizza dotted the floor like a map of the world's continents. It was a first-class horrible mess all right.

"Let's call up some of the guys and get them over to help us clean up," I told Pete. "The two of us will never be able to do it alone."

Pete went off to the phone while I just sat on a cushion that had somehow gotten off the big living room chair and ended up in the middle of the foyer floor surrounded by all sorts of unbreakable junk. I was reminded of the pillow fights Dave and I used to have when we were little kids. We'd start just throwing pillows and pretty soon we were tossing around blankets, socks, books, just about anything we could lay our hands on. But even our best fights never left this kind of mess. I mean, guys even took leaks on the walls. I could see the streaks of urine running down the walls. They were dried up but I could see the marks they left. It was a gross sight.

I was glad when Pete came back to take my mind off the surroundings. "Well?" I asked.

"Nobody'll come over."

"Jeez, Pete, this is too much of a mess for just the two of us to clean up." I got up from where I was sitting. "I'm going home, Pete. Unless you can get some others to help us, I'm out." I started for the front door.

"You have to help, you can't just walk out on me. I'll get killed if this place isn't cleaned up . . ."

Pete's voice came over on a high pitch. *He's beginning to sound like his mother,* I thought.

"Aw, come on," Pete began to coax me, "be a friend."

That really turned me off. He did it to me every time he wanted something. He would start sugaring me up, then end up sticking me with the whole job. Besides, I didn't see how we could ever satisfy his folks.

"I've gotta go do some errands for my mother," I said. I put my hand around the front door knob.

"Cut the crap, Scott. You have to help!" Pete was getting red in the face. He looked awful mad, like a girl getting teased. His dark hair practically covered his eyes. His fists were all rolled up with nowhere to go. So he just stood there hollering and cursing at me. I figured I'd explain how I felt just one more time. I hated to leave him with the whole mess, but he really did deserve it. Friend or no friend I wasn't going to be a jerk just to be nice. Knowing Pete, he wouldn't even say thanks if I did stay.

"Pete, I'm not kidding around. You made more of a mess than anybody else at the party. If you hadn't started tossing drinks at people none of this would've happened." I waved my arm around to take in the whole room.

"You lousy farthead," Pete shrieked at me. "You stink!"

"Look who's talking," I said. I suddenly realized we were beginning to do an imitation of

Pete's folks and that really scared me. I tried to figure out what to say to calm Pete down. But at this point Pete looked ready to kill, so I decided to split before it got any worse. I didn't want to say or do anything to really hurt him.

I pulled open the front door just as Pete was getting ready to send an ashtray at my head.

"Take it easy," I hollered over my shoulder. I quickly pulled the door behind me, just in time to hear the crash of breaking glass.

The further I got from Pete's house the better I felt. Pete had been the worst slob at the party. If he didn't want a mess it was his business to see that the guys acted right. Anyhow that's what I was telling myself as I opened the back door to my house with my key.

The phone was ringing and I rushed into the house to answer it.

It was Pete and he really sounded desperate. "Please, Scott, come on back. I can't take on this whole mess all by myself. Don't be a louse."

I didn't answer him for a minute.

"Listen, you can hear my mother screaming. She's sore as hell at you for leaving," Pete whispered into the phone to me. He was right. I could hear her hollering and it only convinced me even more I better stay just where I was, safe at home.

"Jeez, Pete, I'm not coming back there and have your mother start screaming at me in person. There's just no way I'm going back into your crazy house again while your folks are on the warpath."

Pete kept on whispering to me on the phone. But I was beginning to remember all the other times he had gotten me in trouble with his folks, so I just tuned him out. He had always managed to get his parents to believe anything that happened wasn't his fault by blaming everything on me. And damned if they didn't let him get away with it.

I was beginning to get sore all over again, thinking about all the rotten tricks Pete had pulled on me. I was going to say something, but then I decided there wasn't much point to it. So instead I just said, "Sorry Pete . . . I guess I'll see you in school."

Hanging up on Pete that day was just about the hardest thing I ever had to do. It hurt like hell. But I sure as hell wasn't going back and have his old lady give me the business like she gave Pete. *Wow, what a witch,* I thought. *Pete sure has a tough deal.* I was surprised out of my mind because I always thought he had it so great. *You can't be sure about anything, especially about people and what they're like really,* I thought, knowing even though I had it bad I sure didn't want to change places with Pete now that I knew how he really had it.

I was back to where I started. And there was no one else to go to. I wondered if I could make it on my own. Like go on the road. *Yeah, that's it!* The perfect solution for both of us, Pete and me. We'd take off and go out on our own, away from our folks and everything. He'd love it, I knew. We could both have it made. I began feeling great. Pretty soon all my troubles would be over, and Pete's too.

The school cafeteria was mobbed when I got there. My science teacher had kept me after class for fifteen minutes to explain the difference between meiosis and mitosis. The last chapter on cells and genes and stuff explained both of them okay. But somehow I always got them mixed up with each other when we had a test. Anyhow, that's how come I was late getting to lunch. Which is what made it so tough to find Pete and the rest of the guys I usually ate with.

Then I spotted it. There was Pete's wild scarf flying like a bright skinny flag over the heads of everyone in the place. He was waving it around so I could spot him and the rest of the guys. *What a great mind,* I thought. Pete could be really smart when he wanted to.

I worked my way through to my friends by zigzagging around hundreds of tables and chairs. There were always empty tables pushed into the aisles so that they blocked anybody trying to get by. Like a table that was meant for four people usually ended up with eight people sitting around it. That meant there was another table for four left without any seats. So it usually ended up in the middle of an aisle somewhere. If I didn't get into the cafeteria early it usually meant I'd have to eat standing up or sitting on the edge of an empty table, which was against the school rules. But I took my chances most of the time. There wasn't much choice.

"Here he comes." All the guys got up from the table and started bowing and singing "Allah be praised" to me. That is, everyone who wasn't doing something else like giving me the finger. They sure were a weird lot of great guys.

"How come you're so late, Scott?" a couple of the guys said in unison.

"Maybe he was makin' out with you know who on the stairs again," Steve said. Everybody started making cracks and noises until finally Mr. Finamen, the vice principal, came over and told us to shut up and eat our lunches or get out.

Pete had saved me a seat next to him. I wedged myself in between him and Dean and dropped my notebook and stuff on the table in front of me.

"Aw, shit, Mr. Wyman made me stay after class so he could explain a few things to me."

"You, having problems in bio, Scott? We figured you knew all there was to know about the human anatomy; especially the female human." All the guys were giggling and feeling pretty high. So was I. I didn't mind the guys ribbing me about girls. They were good to look at and what guy didn't think about them? As a matter of fact, most of the guys spent a lot of their time doing just that. Only a couple of the guys in our gang really had steadies or dated many girls. Pete and I had gone out on a couple of dates once or twice but the girls wouldn't even let us kiss them.

"You gotta' be kiddin'. Since when do you learn anything about the human body in bio?" I said. "All we learn about is cells and chromosomes and Mendel's pea. That's spelled p . . . e . . . a."

"Ha ha!" Dean said, "you are real funny today." But his elbow digging into my ribs said otherwise.

"Cut it out, Dean. I have important things to talk about with Pete. So shove it, will you?"

Well, Dean was a good guy, so he crowded closer to the guys on his right and gave me some privacy to talk with Pete.

I looked at Pete to see if he was still sore at me for leaving him with the mess from the party. I figured I'd better say something to cool him down just in case he was still burning over it.

"Look, Pete, I'm awful sorry I left you with that whole mess yesterday. But your folks scared the hell out of me. I didn't want to stick around and take a chance of having to go a second round with them. You know what I mean?"

"Yeah, I know, but you're still a louse for cutting out like that." But the way he was grinning when he said it made me curious.

"So how'd it go? Were you able to get the place cleaned up like they wanted?"

Pete started laughing then. "You wouldn't believe what happened after you left."

I couldn't resist asking, "What?"

"Well, when my folks saw you'd run out on me, they felt so sorry for me they told me not to worry about it. They called up a professional cleaning outfit and got the whole place squared away."

"Boy, are you lucky," I said, knowing I could never have gotten away with anything like that.

"Naw, it's not luck. Whenever my folks bad-mouth me they feel rotten about it. So afterwards they have to try to make it up to me. That's how I get just about everything I want. I just have to wait till they go off the deep end, and I never have to wait too long either . . ." Pete's laughter filled my ears but I could see his eyes weren't smiling.

I decided it was a perfect opening for telling him about my plan.

"Pete, I got a great idea on how we can both fix it so we don't have to listen to our folks ever again."

I began telling him about my great idea when the loudspeaker in the cafeteria started to blare. That thing was so loud I could hardly hear myself think, let alone talk. So I sat back and ate the sandwich I had brought with me from home while I waited for the announcement to end.

". . . and Friday night there will be a dance at the Y's Tub Club . . . magical sounds of Sunny Slope . . . Admission $2.50 per person. Anyone wanting tickets in advance can get them in the school office this afternoon and tomorrow after three o'clock . . . Thank you very much for your attention and have a good day."

"Wow, Sunny Slope. They're terrific!" Dean shouted out, jumping up from his seat. "I'm gonna get my ticket this afternoon before they sell out. How about you guys?" Dean looked around the table at all of us.

"I'll go, too," Pete said.

"Wait a minute, Pete." I was feeling the ground moving out from under my feet and I didn't like it. I didn't want Peter making any plans until he heard me out.

"Come on, Scott," Dean said to me, "they're a great sound, the greatest in fact, and if we all go we could have a ball."

"Yeah, yeah, I know. But I have to discuss something with Pete before I make up my mind."

"Well, come on and walk me to my class and you can tell me your big idea," Pete said, like he was making fun of me to the other guys. He always had to act the big man. Then before I got sore at him I thought, *Aw, what the hell, he can't help it.* Anyhow I was anxious to get him away from the guys so he would get serious.

We got up from the table, signaled good-bye to our buddies, and joined the jam trying to make for the exit. The school building's layout was the result of master planning. All the kids in the school had to be in the cafeteria at practically the same time. Then everybody had to beat it right back to his next class after his lunch hour was over. But there were only two exits and two entrances, one on each side of the room, where people could come and go. The joker was when we all had to stand on line to get lunch and at the end of the line there was only one little old lady who everybody had to pay. What a mess.

Pete and I fought our way out of the cafeteria only to run into another bottleneck going up the stairs. Sometimes I wondered about just how smart the guys were who ran the school. They sure didn't rate too high with me. In fact, Pete and I had decided long before that day that we could do a hell of a lot better at running the school than the principal and his jerky assistants.

I used to think about trying to run for office on the student council but it was always too late when I decided. Anyhow most of the people on the council were creeps . . .

All the way up to Pete's class I told him about how we could go out on our own. He seemed to be listening, but it was hard to tell because we had to spend so much time pushing through people to get moving. But when I finally finished telling Pete, we had reached his classroom.

"Listen, Pete, we could do it. It would solve everything."

"I'm gonna get out, but if I go now my old man won't pay for my education. I want to go to college. After I get that, they'll never see me again . . ."

"You mean you're gonna stick around for another couple of years and keep taking their shit?" Pete couldn't seem to understand what I was saying. I figured if we both ran away together at least one of us could get a job so we could eat and get a place to live. Pete was smart enough to make out no matter what. Between us we'd really be able to have a great time. We could do whatever we wanted and go wherever we wanted . . . It was beautiful.

"Think about it, at least, okay?" I pleaded.

Pete nodded his head, then ducked into his class, closing the door behind him. I could see the teacher look at him through the glass window on the door. Pete was trying not to be noticeable. The teacher was in the middle of saying something. I couldn't hear what he was saying but I was able to figure out that he was pissed off about being disturbed by Pete. All the while Pete was making for his seat the teacher just stood there not saying anything, just watching

Pete move around. Everyone in the class turned his head to watch him. Then damned if Pete didn't trip right over some jerk's pile of books on the floor and practically fall into a girl's lap. She was pretty good-looking, too. I could hear the loud laughter in the room right through the door. Everyone had broken up, except for the teacher, of course. I left to find my class, thinking maybe I could talk Pete into coming along with me after all.

"Scott, I got a letter from Mr. Schmidt today." My mother had the letter in her hand and was giving it to me to read. I knew what it was so I didn't bother to take it.

"Yeah, I know, he's failing me."

"So what are you going to do about it?"

Since I had come home from Pete's, my mother hadn't been around too much, which was great by me. I didn't have to worry about her asking me questions about my homework and stuff like that. And I wasn't going to start talking about it now. I wasn't planning on sticking around much longer and I didn't see any point arguing with her about that creep Schmidt and his rotten algebra course.

I had finally decided to get out of town by myself. Pete was too chicken to come with me. Besides I was tired of trying to make him understand how much better off he would be away from his folks. We had been discussing it for two days and he still couldn't understand what a great idea I had.

I kind of felt sorry for him in a way. He was in a hell of a bag and couldn't seem to break out of it.

My mother was still standing staring at me, waiting for me to say I was sorry or something like I would try to do better. *The hell with that*, I thought. I had enough of school, teachers, mothers, and all the other people who always wanted to butt into my life. I was through waiting forever to be on my own . . .

"Well, Scott," she said again.

"Aw, what the hell difference does it make? Mr. Schmidt's a jerk and doesn't like me, that's all."

"Scott, I've just about had it with you." She threw up her hands like she was really disgusted. "You're going out of your way to mess up your life. And I won't let you do it."

"What do you care? You're so busy dating and working you're never around." I was remembering the creep she had in for dinner the night before. She had been dating a lot of guys since my dad left the house. There was always some guy or other hanging around. It really bugged me. What the hell was my old lady doing messing around with guys, anyhow?

"Scott, I do care. You're my son and I love you." But she sounded more like she'd have liked to kill me just then.

"You're always picking on me. I should've stayed at Pete's house. Why don't you just leave me alone and stop nagging at me?"

I wanted to say a lot more but what was the use. She wouldn't have understood. She would have only started in with me some more.

"I want you to work harder in school. Get some help from Mr. Schmidt so you don't fail this course for the term. You aren't a baby anymore, you know. How you do in high school counts when you apply for admission in college."

"I'm not going to college." I knew that would reach her. She had a thing about education. The secret to all success and happiness and crap like that. Just because she was hung up on education, she expected me to be.

"Well," she said, looking at me like I had my head screwed on sideways, "then you better figure out how you're going to take care of yourself. Because when you stop going to school, you're going to have to start paying your own way."

"I'm not worried," I told her, but I didn't really mean it. I had some big worries. The first was how I could get enough money together to get out of town. Then where would I go? I knew my dad was out. Besides I wanted to be on my own.

I had a friend from camp who lived in Florida and I was thinking about calling him up and seeing if he could put me up for a while. But even if his folks agreed to let me stay there for a while I still needed the travel fare. Yeah, I had real worries. Mr. Schmidt and his math class hardly counted at all.

"Well, Scott, you had better do something and soon," my mother said, not realizing that I was just thinking the same thing. Only the something I was thinking about doing was not the same something she was thinking about.

"Yeah, I guess you're right." But she could see I didn't mean it. That was one thing about my mother. I really couldn't fool her about anything. I wondered how I could get out of the house without her knowing. I decided I'd have to leave while she was out working or out on a date or shopping. I had to make plans, talk to Pete and see if he had any good ideas about where I should go, even though he wasn't going with me. *Maybe,* I thought, *I can still make him change his mind.*

The phone rang and my mother answered it. I just knew it would be Pete. And it was. I ran upstairs so I could talk to him in private.

"Okay, you can hang up now," I hollered down to my mother.

"You coming to the dance on Friday?" Pete said as soon as he heard me answer the phone.

"I told you, Pete, I'm getting out of town." I was getting disgusted with him for not believing me.

"Don't be a jerk, Scott. You don't have it so bad. You're mother is hardly ever around. Anyhow what difference would it make if you stuck around for a couple of more days?" Pete was really giving me a fast sales pitch. He wasn't going to give me a chance to answer him because he went right on talking.

" . . . besides, I heard a couple of terrific girls from Hill High are planning on going . . ."

"Jeez, Pete," I interrupted him, "I don't know." But I was sitting there thinking about it. I was beginning to think that maybe sticking around for a couple more days might not be so bad after all. Then it hit me that it might be a really good deal for me. The day that everybody in the house was usually gone was Saturday. That way, I thought, it would give me a clear field to pack my stuff and get out without anybody making a big scene.

"Well, maybe I will go to the dance," I said, but I tried not to sound too excited. I didn't want Pete to get the idea that maybe I was going to change my mind about leaving.

"Hey, that's great," Pete said. "We'll have a ball." I could hear his brain clicking away like a computer. "Let's get dressed up crazy. I can wear my old man's dress suit and we can find something wild for you."

Pete was being his usual self. He was going to be different from everybody else. He had style. I kind of liked the idea too and began to get caught up in the whole thing. It was fun getting up in some different-looking outfit. One thing was for sure—when we went anyplace, we got noticed. And that wasn't such a bad thing to happen when we went to a dance and wanted to meet new girls. One time Pete wore his old man's dress suit, had his long crazy scarf wrapped around his neck, and a curved wooden cane in his hand and he wore his track sneakers. Nobody missed seeing him that night.

"Okay, I'll go with you Friday. But Saturday I'm really leaving."

"You're crazy, Scott," Pete said like he really wanted to convince me. "You've got a good deal where you are now."

"Hell, no. I've had it with school and parents and being told what to do." Pete didn't want to understand so there wasn't much use trying to make him. Maybe he could stand all the crap that was being dished out to him, but I had had it.

"You got any money, Scott?"

"Yeah, I cleaned up my neighbor's leaves last week and she paid me ten bucks. I've been stashing away any extra money I've been earning for the past couple of months. Why?"

"I just wondered if you had the money to pay back what you owe me . . . you know, the three bucks I loaned you so you could buy that record you wanted."

"Yeah, all right. I'll pay you back tomorrow." Pete was getting to be a real prick.

"I'll see you in the morning. Try to get here on time tomorrow, will you? You want me to call and wake you up?"

I did, but I was sore at him. So instead I said, "Naw, I'll be there. Besides my old lady gets sore when you call up so early."

"Okay, see you . . ." He hung up the phone.

I sat there on my mother's bed thinking about how the whole world stinks when Lisa came into the room.

"You off the phone yet?" she asked.

"You got eyes." I was mad at everybody just then.

"Did you see ma's boyfriend downstairs?" Lisa looked at me like it was a joke or something.

"What boyfriend?"

"That creep she's been dating for the last couple of weeks, dumbhead." Lisa was getting sweeter every day. Boy, I sure felt sorry for any guy who fell for her.

"I didn't see anybody."

"Well, go downstairs and take a look. They're in the den." She started giggling. I couldn't take that so I left her and the phone and went to my room.

"Hey, Dave, did you see ma's boyfriend downstairs?"

Dave was working at his desk for a change. He didn't make it any easier for me with him always plugging away at the books. My mother's standard lecture to me was, "If you ever worked even half as hard as your brother you'd get straight A's." Like I was some kind of genius or something. She was really something. First she told me I'm stupid because I brought home some dumb C. Then she told me how smart I am. Horse shit.

I lay back on my bed and looked at the ceiling. *Everybody stinks.* "Dave, what do you think of ma's new boyfriend? Lisa says he's a creep."

"He's okay," but Dave wasn't really answering my question. That would be just like him. Stay out of it. If it bothered him to see ma going out on dates he'd be the last one to say anything. He was the cool one. He just stayed out of it. Like he used to when dad and ma would fight. As soon as they got started, Dave would go upstairs and he'd stay in our room until it got quiet again.

I decided to look at this guy my mother had downstairs for myself. I went down the stairs slow and easy so I wouldn't make any noise. If I stayed close to the wall the stairs didn't creak as much. I could see into the den from the living room if I stood at a certain angle. I was standing there when my mother spotted me.

"Scott, come in here and meet my friend."

Dammit, who the hell wanted to meet any creepy guy anyway, I said to myself. But I went into the den so she wouldn't make a big deal out of it.

"Scott, this is Joe Cadman." Then she looked at this bearded Joe and said to him, "Scott is quite an artist, too." He nodded. I knew he couldn't care less. Then my mother turned back to me and said, "Joe is a commercial artist, Scott. Maybe he can give you a few pointers."

I nodded just like the bearded creep, who was looking at me like the only points he wanted to give me was to point me out of the room. I didn't feel like staying around anyway so I said, "Nice to meet you," and made a quick exit.

I didn't like the way the guy looked at my mother. Like he wanted to . . . well, like the way I looked at some of the really great-looking broads at school. *My mother was a good-looking woman but that wasn't any reason why she should start acting like a girl,* I thought to myself. After all, I told myself, there was a big difference. She was a mother and mothers didn't act that way. Anyhow I didn't like it at all. I got back upstairs in record time. The house wasn't hot but all of a sudden I felt all sweaty. Like after I did a real fast sixty-yard dash in a race. I was breathing hard and had a knot in my throat.

"Did you see him?" Lisa asked me in a loud whisper, with one of her hands covering the mouthpiece of the phone, as I passed my mother's room.

"Yeah," I mumbled and kept on moving toward my room. Lisa told her friends everything. I wasn't going to give her any more to say. As it was, she told them everything about me because every time they would see me in school they would start in giggling. Like they knew something that would embarrass me. I was studying the ceiling in my room again when Lisa came back into the room. *Privacy is sure nil in this house,* I thought.

"Isn't he awful?" She almost looked upset. "Ma took me out with them last week and he didn't like it at all. He kept trying to get rid of me."

"What does she need that creep for?" I asked more to myself than Lisa.

"She said she has to go out on dates."

"That's nuts." I could see Lisa didn't like the idea of ma out with some jerk any more than I did.

"And you know what else?" she said.

"Hey, would you two guys go into another room to talk? I'm trying to get some work done." Dave never asked anything. He ordered. The big boss.

I decided it might be a good idea to hear what Lisa had to say. So the two of us went into Lisa's room to talk. We sat down on her bed and she started filling my ears up with stuff that made me feel lousy and scared.

Lisa told me how this guy bossed ma around and how she listened to him. She even acted like he was the greatest. What Lisa told me he did was beginning to make me sore. But then I remembered I wasn't going to be around much longer. I wasn't going to have to watch or care that my mother was acting like a jerk over some creep.

"What are we going to do?" Lisa finally asked me.

"What do you mean?" I knew what I was going to do but I couldn't tell Lisa.

Then she asked me, "Do you think they kiss and stuff like that?" I didn't want to think about my mother making out.

"They're too old for that stuff," I told her.

"I bet they do," Lisa was almost fourteen and always pushing romantic stuff. Her nose was always in one of those love story paperbacks. The ones with the gorgeous broad on the cover who has half her dress torn off and a wild, scared look on her face.

"She wouldn't kiss that creep." I was certain.

"Bet they're downstairs doing it right now."

I hated Lisa. "I gotta do my homework." I wanted to get away from her.

"What if ma marries him and he's our stepfather?" Lisa asked as I made it out the door of her room. I didn't answer her.

I got into my room thinking, *It doesn't matter much to me. I'm leaving.* Finally I squeezed my eyes shut trying to close out the picture of my mother with that guy. *She can do whatever she wants. I won't be here to care.* But still the idea of my mother and that guy really burned me up. It wasn't easy to stop caring, I finally decided, as I opened one of my schoolbooks and started doing my homework. At least I knew that it would be the last time I'd have to bother worrying about that shit.

Don't we look great?" Pete asked as we started out of his house. He had on his dad's dress suit and I was in an old business suit of my dad's that he'd left behind. It almost fit me, too. The waist of the pants and jacket were a little too big but my mother sewed in a couple of tucks so the pants wouldn't fall down. My belt covered the tucks and with the jacket unbuttoned no one could tell that it wasn't a perfect fit. I wore my cap and Pete his scarf and we both had our sneakers on. Neither one of us owned a pair of shoes, just sneaks and hiking boots. My mother gave up trying to get me to wear shoes years before when she saw that they just sat in my closet after she would buy them for me.

We got to the dance just after the band started. A wild scene. Just about everybody in town was there. This group really drew a big crowd. Sunny Slope could do no wrong. They had a sound that blew my mind and just about everyone else's who was there listening. The room was quiet, except for their beautiful sound. It was like everyone was holding his breath. No one wanted to miss even one beat.

During the breaks Pete and I wandered around the hall and looked for our buddies. Because of the jam it was hard to find anybody. We decided to break up and try opposite sides of the room. We planned to meet back at the Coke machine as soon as we made the rounds.

I found some of the guys and told them where we'd be. Then I saw Dean. He was with a couple of great-looking girls.

"Hi, Dean, where've you been?" I said as I looked over his friends.

"Hi, Scott, this is Linda, my date, and this is June." June was something else. She was what most guys dream about. Dean's girl was swell but, well, this June had it. She was good looking, really good looking. Her hair was nice and soft and natural. In fact that's what she looked like. Real. I asked her to dance. I'm not the greatest dancer in the world, but the band had started playing a slow melody and I knew all a guy really had to do was hang onto the girl and sway.

"Where do you go to school, June?" I asked. I knew she didn't go to my school. I would have spotted her. I knew that. *Boy, she feels good*, I thought, as we moved around the floor. I felt myself glowing. The sound and the girl. *This is the life.*

"Hill High," she answered.

"Yeah? What class?"

"Junior," she said.

Just like me, I thought, feeling great.

After we finished dancing, I had to show June off to the other guys.

"Hey, Pete," I called, as we got near the Coke machine. Pete was right in the middle of all the guys telling some wild story. Finally the circle broke up with a few hee haws and Pete came over to where we were standing.

"This is Pete, June. Pete, this is June." I felt funny introducing them to each other. I could feel June's body stiffen up a little. Pete looked funny, too. He had a look on his face that told me he was going to say just the wrong thing. So I figured I'd better stop him before he put his foot in it. Pete sure didn't know anything about women. Although he tried. Man, did he try. But nothing.

"Let's split from this place," Pete said. "Nothing's happening around here."

"Are you kidding? Everybody's here. Anyhow, I like the music," I said, tightening my arm around June's shoulders.

"Ah, come on, it's dullsville here. Let's go back to my house and watch the late movie."

"No way, Pete." He could go but I wasn't leaving June for some old movie. "Anyhow, the dance'll be over in another hour. Why don't you stick around till then. Okay?" I figured Pete was just feeling down because he didn't connect with a girl. *Maybe seeing me with June is making him jealous or something,* I thought. Then I got an idea.

"We're gonna walk around. We'll see you later." I left quickly, steering June along before Pete could come up with another argument. He was awful good at finding reasons for things he wanted to do.

There was only another hour left to dance. June had told me she had to get home right after the dance or her mother would get upset. I wasn't going to waste any time arguing with Pete.

We got back onto the dance floor as soon as the music started. "Hey, June, do you have a friend I could introduce to Pete?" I asked.

"Now?"

"Yeah. Maybe if he could connect with someone he wouldn't be so anxious to leave."

"Well," she hesitated.

"He's really a good guy. It's just that he doesn't know how to act with girls. You know what I mean?" I was hoping she would understand and want to help.

"Gee, Scott, I'd like to help you but I don't know if I can get anybody right now." She was looking around the dance floor, like she was trying to spot someone. "There's Margaret. But, she's already dancing with someone. I guess she's out."

I was beginning to wonder if my idea was so good after all. Because now instead of June paying attention to me, we were both busy talking and thinking about Pete.

"Ah, don't worry about it. He'll survive." I must have said something good because June let out a sigh and began to smile at me again.

We spent most of the next hour just talking about school, our folks, and telling stuff about how we felt about things. Pretty soon the music stopped and the crowd was making for the exit. I wanted to stay around until the very last second, or at least as long as June stayed.

"Oh, there's my girlfriend. I guess I'm going to have to leave now, Scott. I really had a lovely time tonight. Thanks a lot." She smiled at me.

"Why don't you let me walk you home?" I asked. I had another idea growing in my head and needed more time to get my nerve up.

"Well, I'd like that. But would you mind terribly walking my friend home, too?"

"Okay by me. But let's walk her home first." I really wasn't asking. I felt good seeing how fast she agreed with me.

"What about your friend Pete?" she asked, ripping up my beautiful plan. *Dammit*, I thought, *sometimes Pete* . . . I stopped the words in my head. They made me feel like an awful louse. After all, Pete was my best friend.

He'd been around with me since we both first started to walk. He was closer to me than my brother. But I wasn't happy about him coming along with June and me right then.

June's friend came over to us and June introduced her to me. I nodded, still worrying about what to do about Pete.

Then I found out June was not only beautiful, she was smart, too.

"Margaret," June said to her friend, "Scott and Pete are going to walk us home, okay?"

Margaret nodded.

"Good." June smiled at her. "Since I have to get right home, Pete will take you and Scott will take me. You know how my mother is." Margaret, the living doll, agreed. Now all I had to do was convince Pete.

"I'll be right back. Wait right here," I told the girls. I made my way over to Pete.

"Boy, it's about time you got over here." Pete was sulking.

"Jeez, Pete, stop getting all overheated. I just made a terrific deal for you."

"Big deal. What is it?"

"See the girl with June over there?"

"Yeah? So what about her?"

"She's really great," I said, hoping I sounded convincing.

Pete was getting impatient. "Let's go, Scott. Maybe we can make the rest of the late movie if we move fast."

"Never mind the movie. I made a connection for you. You're gonna walk her home."

"You're nuts. I'm not walking some girl home."

"Come on, Pete, don't be a chickenshit. Look at her, she's really good looking. Come on, give it a chance."

Pete looked at her again. Then he looked back at me and his lip was curled up on one side of his mouth. He smelled something phony. Damn smart ass could always read me.

"Hey, girls," I hollered before Pete could make any moves, "come over here." The place was almost empty now and my voice sounded kind of hollow. Or maybe it was just that I was feeling stretched out.

"Margaret, this is my great buddy, Pete."

Pete grinned silly and looked like he couldn't think of anything to say. That was different for him. I figured maybe he thought Margaret wasn't so bad after all.

"Pete, you're walking Margaret home while I take June to her house. I'll meet you back at your house later." Pete grinned a different grin at me then. It was pure hate. He was sore as hell at me. There wasn't a thing he could do about it right then because I grabbed June's arm and headed to where we had stashed our coats.

"See you in a little while," I shouted back at Pete. He looked like a scared little kid. It sure was funny about Pete. He could be the wisest wise ass in the place but when it came to girls . . .

"Why are you shaking your head?" June asked me as she put on her hat and coat.

"Pete. I'm thinking about how scared he is of girls. He's got five sisters, too. Weird, that's what it is," I said.

June smiled at me. I felt warm all over. There was a strange tingle in the bottom of my stomach. *Man,* I thought, *it's a good thing she can't read what's in my head right now.*

The weather had turned real cold that day. The night was even colder. But the stars were all out bright and clear. The moon lit up the street better than the street lights. I had my arm tight around June's waist. She was getting a red nose and her body was kind of hunched down to keep the cold out. We walked fast.

"Hey, June, how about going out with me next Saturday?" The words came out fast. I could see my breath hanging in the cold air. I guess I was hanging in the cold air too, waiting for her to answer. I was scared.

"Oh, Scott, I'm sorry. I have a date next Saturday." There was a frown between her eyes like she really meant it.

"Really?" I asked her, but not believing her.

"Yes. I'm sorry," she whispered back.

There wasn't anything else to talk about after that. I just wanted to get her home fast and beat it. I wanted to kick myself for asking her out. It had taken all my nerve. Dammit, I couldn't figure out why she didn't like me. I was all mixed up and felt terrible.

"Scott, I hope you'll call me sometime," she said when we got to her house. She looked straight into my eyes. I wanted to run and hide so I could cry.

"Yeah, sure I'll call you." But I didn't want to look at her anymore let alone call her.

She told me to wait a second while she went inside the house. She brought back a piece of paper and wrote her telephone number on it.

"Here," she said, as she handed me the paper. "And thanks again for a wonderful evening. 'Bye," she sort of sang out to me as I started down the block away from her house. I knew I wasn't going to go over to Pete's feeling so lousy. He'd have me spilling my guts and then he'd torture me about it for the rest of my life. *No sir,* I thought, *I'm going home and start packing so I can get going first thing tomorrow.* I'd call Pete from home and tell him I wasn't coming over. I had to think. I wanted to be alone to do it.

It seemed like a guy always ended up by himself one way or the other. I was glad that Dave was out when I got back home. Lisa was sleeping. My mother must've been on one of her dates. That thought made me feel even lousier. I went up to my room and dragged out my duffle bag. But after a while I just found myself sitting on my bed, staring at the still empty bag. I decided to go to sleep and get up early and pack. I was feeling beat. I lay down on my bed and thought about what had just happened to me.

It had been a wild time. I flew higher than ever before in my life. A natural high, it was called. But it sure wasn't worth getting high like that if I got the low that I felt when I came down.

I decided never to get caught on an updraft like that again. No girl was worth it. I stopped myself from thinking about that sweet face and soft body. *Dammit,* I thought, punching my pillow, *what can a guy do?* It seemed that everything always turned out rotten for me. I began thinking about how it was going to be after I went out on my own the next day. Maybe then things would change for me. But somehow, I didn't feel like they would.

I had looked at myself in the bathroom mirror when I got back home that night. What I saw made me understand why June turned me down. I guess I couldn't really be mad at her for not wanting to go out with a creep like me.

But that didn't make it any better. I still hurt bad. *Tomorrow,* I thought, half asleep, *I'll get away from it all.*

What are you doing?" Dave asked me as I was stuffing some clothes in my duffle bag. He had been sleeping and I figured I could pack and leave before he woke up. My mother had left for work while I was still asleep. I was glad I wouldn't have to see her.

"How come you're not working today?" I was sore at him for being around to bother me, asking questions when he wasn't supposed to be.

"I switched hours with a friend of mine." Then after a few seconds more of watching me he said, "Can't you do that later on so I can sleep?"

"Don't worry, in a little while I won't be around here to disturb you or anybody else for that matter." I shoved in a pair of old jeans, making the side of the bag bulge out peculiarly. I wondered about whether I should take my good jacket, too. I wasn't sure where I was going yet so it was tough to decide just what to take with me. I ended up just putting in anything of mine I could find that was clean.

"What're you crabbing about now?" Dave had a disgusted look on his face. He didn't like being annoyed when he wanted to sleep.

"I'm leaving town. I'm getting away from all of you so you won't have me around to boss . . . you and ma . . . even dad . . . none of you give a damn for or about me . . . so I'm going out on my own." That really woke him up. He sat up in his bed.

"Did you talk to ma about this?" Dave asked me.

"Are you kidding? When is she ever around? Even when she is around, she's got no time to talk to me. She's too busy with her jobs and boy-friends." I could feel all the anger coming up into my throat. The taste of tears was in my mouth.

Dave was shook up by then. He looked kind of puzzled. He had that old man look on his face. I guess it was hard for him, being the older brother. He seemed to think he had to know more than the rest of us. At least he tried to act that way.

"Listen, Scott, you better wait until ma gets back."

"I'm not waiting. I'm going now."

"You know you're crazy, don't you? Ma really loves all of us. And she worries a lot about you. She's always talking about you to me. All the time you were at Pete's house she had Lisa and me watching out to make certain that you got to school and you looked okay and stuff like that." Dave was talking more than ever before. It sounded strange to hear him like that. All rushed and wordy. He wasn't taking time to think like he usually did before he talked.

"How come she never talks to me then?" I asked him.

"Why don't you ask her that?" Dave answered.

But I thought about what he was saying. *My mother was worried about me.* Sure, but that was because she figured I wasn't smart enough to take care of myself. It didn't matter anyhow, because I was going to take off. Then she wouldn't have to worry about me anymore.

My bag was just about as stuffed up as I could get it and still be able to close the zipper. I wanted to take my radio clock with me but I decided it would be too much added weight to carry. Besides, once I got away I wouldn't need to know what time it was. I'd never have to hear the alarm waking me up in the morning so I could get to school on time. That gave me a good feeling.

"Scott, you better not do anything crazy." Dave was out of his bed and following me around the room in his bare feet while I made sure I had everything I would need.

"I'm through listening to all that stuff. There's nothing to stick around here for." And a flash picture of that pretty little face lit up in my head, making me move faster.

Dave followed me around as I got my stuff out of the bathroom, talking a mile a minute. I supposed he was scared ma would blame him for my running away.

By the time we got downstairs and into the kitchen Dave had grabbed hold of my arm and started to drag me over to the wall phone.

"I'm going to call ma up and you can talk to her." His arm was crooked tightly around my neck. I was getting madder than hell and trying every wrestling trick I knew to get loose from him. But Dave was dragging me across the kitchen floor like I was a sack of garbage.

The phone rang.

We both jumped at the sound and Dave let me go.

I guess I answered the phone because I couldn't help it. Whenever I heard that ring my body moved like I was plugged into the phone wire or something. Once our science teacher was discussing some psychology stuff about a Russian scientist who could make dogs feel hungry just at the sound of a bell. That was me, the sound of a bell set me off so that I had to answer the phone.

"Scott, is that you?" the husky mumbling on the other end of the phone told me Pete had just gotten up out of bed.

"Yeah, it's me." I didn't want to talk to him. He gave me a hard enough time last night when I had called him and told him I wasn't coming over to his house. I didn't want to answer any more of his stupid questions.

"Whatcha' doin'?" Pete asked.

"Packing."

"Huh?"

"Don't act so stupid, stupid. I told you I was taking off today." I wanted to hang up and get going. But even though I knew I should hang up on him, I just couldn't do it.

"I bet Juney girl turned you down, right?" Then he started to laugh like he knew something I didn't know. He wouldn't have dared to laugh like that if we were in the same room together. Pete was brave and mean so long as he knew I couldn't reach him to smash in his face.

"You want to get your head broken?"

"Tell the truth, Scott. What happened last night?"

"Whatdya mean what happened? I just took the girl home, that's all." I tried to make my voice sound like I didn't care. But it was impossible. I couldn't fool somebody I just about lived with all my life.

"Did you ask her for a date?"

That damn creep. He never let up. I had to

be careful not to say anything that would give him the laugh on me.

"Why would I ask June for a date, you ass? I was planning on getting lost today, remember?"

"Yeah, I guess so." But Pete didn't sound too convinced. "Why don't you come over here before you head out?"

I agreed to stop by his house before I got started to get him off my back. But there was another reason, too. I still didn't know where I was going. I had thought about standing on the highway and getting a hitch anywhere the driver was going. I really didn't care where I ended up. I knew I didn't have enough money to get along for very long. But I figured it would be easy to pick up a job washing dishes or something as soon as I got someplace. Going over to Pete's would give me a chance to work out a plan. He usually came up with bright ideas when he was in the mood. Anyhow, I wasn't in that big a hurry to leave town. In fact I was feeling kind of scared and worried about the whole thing now that I had really decided to leave.

Dave was standing there watching me. I could tell he was listening to me talking to Pete. He didn't leave my side. He wasn't going to take any chances I would get away before he could call my mother. So when I hung up the phone he grabbed my arm and I knew he wasn't going to let me go until I did what he wanted.

"What's all that stuff about last night?" Dave asked. "Didn't you go to a dance with the guys?"

"Yeah." I could see his head was working overtime.

"Who's June?" Dave asked me so suddenly that it didn't give me a chance to think of anything original.

"Just a girl I met at the dance last night."

Then something happened that blew my mind. I knew we lived in a small town. But I never really believed it was that small. I remembered my mother telling me that we lived in the kind of town where if we didn't want the neighbors to know our business we had better do it out of town. Was she ever right.

"Scott's in love with her." Dave and I both jumped at the sound of Lisa's voice. She was in the den watching TV or rather listening to us in the kitchen. She had heard everything that went on.

"Shut up, Lisa!" But I knew that she wouldn't. Even if I told her I didn't want anybody to know, she'd manage to blab her mouth off to somebody. She didn't know what a secret was. If Dave wasn't hanging onto me I would have gone into the den and put my fist down her big mouth.

"Dave, ask him about how he was dancing all night and never letting go of her hand. They were making cow eyes at each other." And she started to giggle like mad. Then she started singing some stupid song about love and kissing and shit like that.

"I'm gonna kill you," I hollered at her, really meaning it. Then I began to wonder how she knew so much about what happened to me. "Who told you all that stuff, anyway?"

That question got her up and brought her into the kitchen with Dave and me.

"Dean's sister." Then I remembered Dean had a dumb sister the same age as mine. They were friends. "And she told me you asked June for a date and she turned you down."

"How could she know that?" I asked Lisa, my blood frozen cold inside my skin because I knew the answer before she told me.

"Dean's girlfriend is June's best friend and she called June after you took her home. That's how."

Holy Jeez, that meant Dean's girlfriend called Dean and told him what June did to me. Dean knew June had turned me down. Maybe that's what Pete was laughing about. Dean probably told him about it already. That's probably why Pete wanted me to stop by his place before I left town, to razz me.

If ever I had a reason for leaving town I had one then. I could never face the guys, knowing they knew what had happened to me. It was a good thing I had planned on going before the dance. I felt terrible. All the guys knowing how I was turned down. I could have died.

"Just a second," Dave stopped Lisa from going on with her story. "What do you mean she turned Scott down?"

Lisa was only too happy to tell him. She was

all smiles like she felt so smart. I wanted to crown her one.

"Scott asked June for a date and she told him she was busy." She really looked proud of herself. The big-mouthed brat.

"Scott, is that what happened?" Dave looked at me like he had a brainstorm or something.

"Yeah," I answered, but I couldn't look at him when I said it. I wished they would all disappear and let me alone. I pulled away from Dave's hold on me and walked over to where my duffle bag lay on the floor. I bent down to pull it up. It felt like it weighed a ton.

"Did she say she didn't want to go out with you or that she was just busy?" Dave sounded like one of those TV lawyers questioning the witness in court.

"What difference does that make?" I said, not wanting to remember the bad scene.

"A big difference, dummy."

"Whatdya mean?" I looked right at Dave then. I didn't like being called dummy, but there was something about the way he said it that made me want to hear more.

"Did it ever occur to you that maybe the girl was really busy?" He had an "aren't I brilliant?" look on his face. I turned my eyes away so I didn't have to see him looking at me like I was some kind of weird jerk.

"Then why didn't she say she'd see me another time?" I half mumbled the question under my breath. But then I remembered she gave me her phone number like she really wanted to hear from me again. I looked back at Dave and wondered if it was possible. If June was really busy and would see me some other time.

He must've read my mind because he said, "You'll never know if you don't call her and ask her if she wants to go out with you some other time." Dave was not the kind of guy who would tell anybody to do something he thought might be wrong. He was careful about being right. That's what made him seem so cool all the time. He never talked unless he was sure he had something important to say.

"What if she turns me down again?" I was scared, but now I didn't mind if Dave knew. He seemed okay to me then. Like he really did care about me.

"The worst that'll happen is she'll say no. And I'm betting she won't. You know she could have been telling the truth."

I thought about that for a second or so. Dave was right about that. June sure did seem like a right girl, not a tease or bitch type. She came on straight with me, but . . .

"Call!" Dave commanded. He looked so certain about it I decided I would take a chance.

"Okay, but the two of you scram outa' here."

"No, you scram," Lisa, my dear sensitive sister, screamed at me. But she went back into the den to watch the TV or, more like it, to spy on me some more.

"I'll call from upstairs," I screamed back. And before I lost my nerve I ran out of the kitchen and up the stairs to my mother's room.

Of course when I got up there I remembered I had left June's phone number in my coat pocket. I was glad I hadn't torn it up and thrown it away like I was tempted to do after I left her at her house.

I ran back downstairs to the den where I had left my coat the night before.

"Well, what did she say?" Lisa asked. Dave, who was in the den, too, sitting on the sofa looked away from the TV at me.

"Jeez, you two, I didn't even call yet." And I beat it out of there and back upstairs. I sat on my mother's bed trying to get back my breath and some of the nerve I had on the first run upstairs. I finally decided if she turned me down again it wouldn't matter anyway because all the guys knew already and besides I was leaving town.

It was the toughest phone call I ever made in my life. I pushed the buttons slow and hard and I wished with all my might that she would be the one to answer the phone. If she wasn't there, I doubted I'd wait around to call again.

"Hello," she said in that musical way. *She even sounds pretty,* I thought.

I cleared my throat before answering. I could feel all the words scrambled up inside my head.

"June, is that you?" *What a jerk I must sound like asking such a stupid question.*

"Scott, is that you?" The way she said it sounded like she was saying, "Scott, I hope that's you."

"Yeah, it's me. How are you?"

"Fine, and you?"

I guess we were both stalling for time. I knew I was. Then I decided to plunge right in the way we had to in swim class when we knew the water would be freezing but the faster we got in and moving the faster we'd warm up.

"Hey, June, I was wondering . . ."

"What, Scott?"

Gee, I like the way my name sounded when she said it. I could feel a grin on my face. I felt like I was drunk or something.

"You said you were busy next Saturday. I was wondering if you would like to go out with me the weekend after that. Like on a Saturday night or something . . . we could go to a movie or something . . ." I was rattling away, and feeling more stupid than ever when she finally interrupted me.

"I'd love to." Just like that, simple and quick.

"You would?" I swallowed hard. She would. She really liked me. That great chick really liked me enough to go out with me. Damn, I felt like I was flying or something. I didn't want to hang up.

She was beautiful to talk to even on the phone. It was like we knew each other for years. We had so much to talk about. I lay back on my mother's pillow with the phone resting against my ear and just listened to her voice. I could picture her face in my head and almost felt her body there on the bed next to me. I tingled all over.

"You must've been on that phone for two hours," Lisa said to me when I finally got back downstairs. I was feeling so good I didn't care what she said.

"Well?" Dave looked at me, smiling. "I guess I was right."

"I've got a date with her the week after next."

"Big deal," my sweet kid sister said, but I could see she loved it.

"That's great," Dave said, and he looked like he really meant it. He was happy for me.

"Now that you've decided to stay around for a while longer, you better get all that gear you stashed in your duffle bag back in the closet and drawers before ma comes home."

Dave looked so proud of himself just then I didn't have the heart to argue with him for bossing me around again. But I did know one thing. He was right about my sticking around for a while.

I got my duffle bag from the kitchen and pulled it back upstairs to my room. While I got my junk out of the bag and was putting it away I wondered how I was going to stop Pete from kidding me for not leaving like I said I was. I thought about that real hard. At least the guys couldn't give me the business about June. That was a relief. But Pete could always find something to pick on.

I wondered whether I should tell Pete about my date with June. I knew I'd have to play it real cool. I wasn't going to have him get anything on me. Then I thought maybe I should call Dean and let him know about my date with June. *The hell with it,* I thought, as I put the last of my clothes away. *They'll probably hear about it through the grapevine anyway.*

I was beginning to feel pretty good again, thinking maybe things could work out after all. But then I saw Mr. Schmidt's letter to my mother on top of my desk and remembered if I stayed around I would have to keep going to his class. Then it hit me. If I wanted to date June I was going to need some way to get hold of steady money. After all a guy couldn't do anything, like take a date to a nice place, without money.

I threw the empty duffle bag back into my closet and tried to figure out what I was going to do about everything if I stuck around.

I wondered why it seemed every time I wanted something it was so tough to do. I wondered if things got easier for a guy when he got older. I sure hoped like the devil they did because just then there didn't seem to be anything but problems for a guy like me.

*H*aving a real girlfriend made me feel very different about what a girlfriend really was supposed to be to a guy. I used to have a girlfriend named Shirley a couple of years ago. It was dumb kid stuff. We used to go over to the cemetery and make out behind the tombstones. I wouldn't call her a girlfriend the way I'd call June though. Then there was Linda, but she was more like a buddy than a girl. We used to do a lot of easy talking about sex together and she was a good sport. But being with her was like being with Pete—although she told me a lot about girls that even Pete, with all his sisters running around his house, didn't know a thing about. But I still can't say she was a real girlfriend.

June was more of an all around friend than Linda and better at making a guy feel like floating than Shirley. But of course, I was only a kid when I went with Shirley. Anyway, after June and I had our first date life sure did change for me in a lot of ways. The world didn't seem to be so stupid to me anymore. Like now I was doing things I used to think only the jerks did.

I was lying on my bed thinking about how things had changed for me since I met June. Like, right then I was waiting for her to come over to my house so we could do our homework together. It was really something. Me, waiting and willing to do my homework. *What a terrific girl,* I thought, remembering how she made it all happen.

We had just gotten out of a really rotten movie and were walking home one Saturday night trying to figure out what made the picture so lousy. I don't know what I said to set her off but all of a sudden June stopped walking and pulled me around by my hand so we were facing each other.

"You know, Scott, you're really a very smart person. You always manage to put your finger on just the right points whenever we're discussing something."

I stood there grinning like an ape, loving every word. Naturally I wasn't going to interrupt her.

"So tell me, why aren't you pulling top grades in school?"

"Hey, wait a minute . . ." I wasn't going to get into that kind of a discussion. But she didn't let me stop her from going on.

"You're as smart as I am, maybe even a little bit smarter. And if I can get A's I don't see why you can't. Besides, I'd feel awfully proud of you if you came out top in your class."

June's dark brown eyes seemed to be looking right into my brain. There was a little frown on her face and I knew she wouldn't let me joke my way out of this conversation.

"Aw, June, what's the point . . ." I started to say. Sure she got A's, but she worked hard for them. I wasn't about to knock my brains out for nothing.

"The point is, you *are* very smart, and you're wasting your time and brains. And that's terrible. Besides, I think it's acting like a baby."

"Come on, June. Stop getting so serious."

"You come on, Scott. How do you think I feel having the class clown for my boyfriend? And what hurts more than anything is I know you're not like that at all. What's the matter with you? Why must everyone think you're something you're not?"

She was really pouring those words out on me. I could see she was getting worked up.

"All right, take it easy. Just what do you want me to do about it?"

"I want you to make a promise to me that you'll do your homework every day for the next two months."

"Every day? Hey, that's ridiculous . . ."

"Promise me."

Well, of course I promised. After all what could a guy do when the girl he wants to kiss good-night is standing there wasting precious time on unimportant things.

It turned out to be a pretty good idea after all. Mostly because June promised in exchange for my doing my homework every day, she'd come over to my house and do her homework at the same time. It certainly beat having to wait for the weekends to get to see her.

Of course, June saw to it I really did do my homework before we could fool around or anything. After a couple of weeks I was almost enjoying the idea of having homework to do. The two months went by awful fast and I was still working away like it had become a habit or something.

Anyway, doing the stuff every day must've made the difference because I was beginning to pull A's in math. And, boy, did I ever get a kick out of Mr. Schmidt. He kept staring at me during class like he never saw me before. I was really getting that bugger crazy. Now he had to pass me and it must've been killing him.

"Dave, you gonna be going to work today?" Dave was sitting at his desk studying. Now there was a guy who knocked himself out to make a mark. I couldn't understand it either. It wasn't like anybody was forcing him. In June's house, her mother got hysterical if she didn't pull an A.

But Dave, with no one pushing him, just kept plugging away.

"Uhmmm . . ." he answered me. I didn't understand him, of course. He had a habit of mumbling so I would never figure out if he said yes or no.

"Are you or aren't you?" I sat up on my bed and turned around to look at him.

"What are you talking about, Scott? Can't you see I'm studying?" He waved his hand at me like he was waving a fly away.

"Are you or aren't you going to work today?"

"No."

"How come?"

"I have to study for mid-years. They're coming up next week."

"Jeez, it seems like you just started your term. We don't get our mid-years for another month."

"College terms are shorter."

"Yeah, I guess so." I said, but I was thinking of something else. Like how was I going to get Dave out of the room when June came over. *Dammit, there isn't a private spot in the whole house,* I thought to myself. I could hear Lisa giggling in her room with her girlfriends. And they wouldn't stay put. They'd probably be in the den watching TV just when I'd want to use it.

There just didn't seem to be any place where June and I could be alone. Her house was impossible. Her mother was a nervous wreck and didn't leave us alone for a second. If we were up in June's room we had to leave the door open. Even so, she would pop in and out of the room every two seconds.

The only chance we ever had to be alone was when Dave was at work. I was still sore because he didn't live at the college dorm. But my mother decided she couldn't afford to pay dorm fees so that meant Dave had to commute to college and live with us at home. I couldn't figure out why he didn't seem to mind. After all if I didn't have any privacy, neither did he. He was weird. Even when I was in the room with him he could act as though I weren't. He just didn't care, I guess. But then he didn't have a steady girl either. I wished he had one. That way he would've understood why I needed some privacy.

"Ah, hell, Dave, couldn't you at least take a break or disappear or something for an hour or so today so June and I could have the room for ourselves?"

I was pleading with him and I could hear the whine in my voice. It made me feel kind of sore at myself, making noises like a little kid. But it was important. If only I could convince Dave how important. But it wasn't any use talking to him.

"Why don't you go downstairs?"

"Naw, Lisa and her jerky friends will be all over the place."

"Go over to June's," Dave suggested like he couldn't care less, because right after he said it he went back to his studying. I saw there was no point arguing with him because he was just going to make like I wasn't there. He was terrific at ignoring people, especially me.

The worst thing about it was my mother told me I'd have to get used to things the way they were.

"We're staying right here until you and Lisa graduate from high school. Dave will have to stay until he finishes his sophomore year in college."

She told me that when I was fighting with her one night about getting a room of my own. I figured maybe she could push up the roof and make a room up there. A friend of mine got his own room that way. But my mother said, "No way, no money."

That meant I was going to have this problem for another two years. *Man,* I thought, *there just must be something I can do . . .*

The doorbell rang.

I raced down the stairs. It was June. She smiled at me that sweet smile that could turn the solid mass that was my body into pure hot liquid.

Wow.

"There's just no place for us to be alone."

June and I were sitting in the kitchen. We were trying to figure out some way we could find a place to be alone. We'd been talking about it for more than half an hour and getting nowhere when down came Dave for something to eat. He got some stuff from the refrigerator and sat down at the table with us. We just sat there watching while he stuffed his face. He wasn't self-conscious like I would've been having people staring at me while I ate.

Then June's brains and sweetness combined to come up with the answer.

"Dave, can't you help us find some place in the house to be alone so we can get some work done?"

Now, even cold Dave couldn't resist a face like June's, which, when she set her mind to it, could probably melt a glacier. At least, it sure made me hot.

And it worked. Dave stopped eating long enough to think. *He can only do one thing at a time*, I thought to myself, mad because he would listen to June but not to me. *Jeez, I'm jealous of my own girl.*

"Well," Dave said, like he'd been puzzling over the problem for years, "the only thing I can think of as a possibility is to make a room in the basement. That is, if ma will let you." He said that looking straight at me.

He knew that would be the problem, too. Ever since dad had moved out, ma had turned real cheap. She wouldn't spend a penny unless she thought it was absolutely necessary. And somehow the only necessities were what she wanted. But Dave's idea was good. And I decided to think about it.

"Let's go downstairs now and take a look," June said, smiling at me.

I took her hand and we opened the door to the basement. There was a switch on the top of the stairs that turned on a kind of dim light downstairs. The steps were just wooden slabs and the railing wasn't too sturdy. It moved if I pulled down on it. In other words, I could see right away what a big job it was going to be if we decided to use the basement.

And was it a mess. There wasn't a spot without something on it, a box of junk or an old appliance or a broken piece of furniture. Then I spotted something which told me maybe it just might be done. In the far right-hand corner I saw a batch of two-by-fours perfect for me to use in dividing up the basement.

"Hey June," I said, hugging her because I took every chance I could to get real close. "I think we can do it. All I have to get is some plywood and maybe some paneling."

"But Scott," she said, looking around, "there's no place that I can see for you to put a room in all this mess."

Now June was smart about some things but she tended to get discouraged pretty easy. I figured it must've been something she learned from her folks. In her family nobody was ever encouraged no matter how good they were. In fact, June's folks were not too happy because June was determined to go to college and make something of herself. Her mother was a real pill. She didn't make any sense to me. Even though she wanted June to get A's in school, the only thing she had in mind for June's future was marriage and babies. She couldn't understand why June didn't want to have the same kind of life she had. Which was funny because she acted so miserable and unhappy with her husband. Once in a while I found myself getting nervous, because her mother looked at me like I was going to be the guy June was going to marry. June said her mother was crazy and not to worry about her. But I noticed she never broke any of her mother's rules. Anyway, I figured it was a good idea to stay away from June's mother as much as possible, just in case she was getting the wrong ideas in her head about me.

June's mother was certainly the opposite of mine. Mine was always telling us kids we could do or be anything we wanted if we really wanted to work for it. Sometimes I wondered about that, especially when I'd work my balls off for something and it didn't happen. Her answer was I just hadn't worked hard enough. What the hell. But I really did want that room and there was just no way I wasn't going to work like hell to get it. That much I knew.

"We'll just throw the junk out."

"Will your mother let you do that?"

"Sure, why not? She never uses any of this junk." But I was wondering if she was going to make her usual stink about anything I wanted to do.

"Oh, Scott, wouldn't it be great to have our own room?" Her eyes were wide open and deep brown. She had the prettiest, straightest little teeth and her hair was the same color as her eyes, a kind of soft-looking brown frame for her face. She looked so happy and excited I just wanted to put my arms around her and have her close by me forever. Jeez, she made me feel great.

"We'll have it. I'll start on it right after I get back from work Saturday." I had a job washing dishes at a hamburger joint Friday and Saturday afternoons. It wasn't much of a job but at least I had some steady money coming in. June had a job, too. She made more money than me so we usually went out dutch. She was a good kid. She was a terrific friend, too. Not just a girlfriend but a buddy I could count on. Like the time Pete and I went on a trip to New York City for a couple of days and she loaned me the money. She was a good kid. I wanted her to come, too, although Pete sure didn't. But it didn't matter because her mother put up a real stink and she couldn't go.

"You working this whole weekend?" I asked, because June had a boss who would've made her work every day if he could.

"Well, I kind of promised I might work on Sunday." She was the sort of person who hated to say no.

"Tell your boss you've got something else to do."

"But Scott . . ."

"Listen June, you've got to learn not to let people step on you."

"I know you're right. But I did kind of say yes already about this weekend . . ." She looked so upset I decided not to bug her about it, but it sure made me sore. Every time we planned something together it was either her mother or her boss getting in the way.

"Well, try to get off so we can work on the room together. At least on Sunday . . . okay?"

She nodded her head with a sad look on her face. So I gave her a quick kiss on the cheek and squeezed her around the waist a little. We went back up to the kitchen just like that. All the way up those rickety stairs I kept my hand holding her close to me around her little waist. She was so little I could circle her waist with my two hands touching each other.

We didn't do much homework that afternoon. Mostly, we planned on what we wanted the room to be like. We were so busy talking and planning we never noticed the time. But her mother sure did. Right on the button. Six o'clock she called up screaming for June to get on home.

When I got back from walking June home I saw my mother's car in the driveway.

"Hi, Scott. Have a good day, dear?" My mother was busy cutting some lettuce into the salad bowl. I walked over and pulled out a piece and stuffed it into my mouth. All of a sudden I remembered I hadn't eaten since lunchtime and I was awfully hungry.

My mother must've read my mind because she barely looked up from what she was doing and said, "Dinner will be ready in ten minutes. Go wash up." I started to move out of the room. "Scott," she called out after me, "Pete called while you were out and wants you to call him right back."

"I'll call him from upstairs. Holler up to me when dinner's ready, okay?"

My mother shook her head like she meant no, but she said, "All right, but don't let the food get cold."

"Whatdya say ol' buddy?" I was lying down on my mother's bed with my feet hanging over the edge so I wouldn't dirty her cover. She always made such a damn big fuss if she caught me with my shoes on her bed. It was so stupid, too. She took the cover off when she went to sleep anyhow. Women sure were screwy sometimes.

"I got a great idea for us."

Pete's voice was all excited. It was catching because I could feel myself getting excited and I didn't even know what he wanted to tell me.

"My sister and her boyfriend are biking up to the Cape this weekend." Pete stopped talking for a minute like he was waiting for me to say something.

"Yeah?"

"Well, guess what?"

"Come on, Pete. Stop being a creep."

"We can go along with them. Wouldn't that be great?"

I thought about that for a minute and remembered how we were always talking about taking an overnight trip on our ten-speeds but it always fell through. Usually because my mother was scared of letting me go alone with Pete.

"Jeez, Pete," and now I could feel myself getting really excited, "that would be a great trip to take."

"Yeah, and Tom, my sister's friend, has done it before. He's twenty-two, so your old lady shouldn't be able to make a stink this time."

"Wow, yeah, great. I mean, yeah." I could picture us on our bikes. The early sharp spring wind making our hair fly back and our eyes slitted so that we could keep the dust and wind from blinding them. "It's great. When are we leaving?"

"We're starting out Friday right after we get back from school."

"Jeez," I thought aloud about my boss, "I'll ask one of my buddies to fill in for me at work over the weekend."

"Good. You better figure on bringing some warm clothes; money too. It's still too cold to plan on sleeping out. We're not gonna carry too much stuff. Just sleeping and emergency gear. We'll eat our meals out, and use the youth hostels along the way."

Pete and I talked like that until I heard my mother hollering about dinner getting cold.

"I better get off. I'll call you later." I hung up the phone and went down to dinner.

That night Pete and I planned all the details. During dinner I told my mother about the trip and she said it sounded great to her. So I was all set.

I got into bed that night after I spent an hour or so rummaging around for my bike gear. I had bought a repair kit for my bike but had put it away because I didn't want to leave it on the bike when I used it. It would have gotten ripped off for sure. In fact, when I took my bike into town and left it while I went into the store to shop, I always carried my front wheel with me, even though I locked the bike. I had spent two years saving for that bike and I was damned if anybody was going to rip me off. An awful lot of guys I knew had it happen to them. I wasn't taking any chances.

I was lying in bed thinking about all the gear I needed to pack into my saddle bags when I looked up at my tack board and saw June's picture on the wall.

Holy Christ, I thought suddenly, *I forgot all about the basement room.* I could feel a flash of adrenaline spill through my whole body in an instant. I had remembered what I had promised June that afternoon down in the basement. How the hell was I going to go on the bike trip with Pete and fix up the room, too? I threw myself over on my stomach, hating me most of all. How did I always manage to get into such rotten fixes? What was I going to do if June asked for and got the weekend off from her job?

Jeez, things were always so damn complicated for me. All I ever tried to do was have a little fun and nothing ever went right. *What am I gonna do about this mess,* I thought. *Somebody is bound to end up sorer than hell with me.* That much I could figure out real fast.

Whatdya mean you can't go?"
Pete looked madder than hell and I couldn't
really blame him. We were walking home after
school and I had finally gotten up enough nerve
to tell him I wasn't going on the bike trip with
him.

"I just forgot all about something I was
gonna do, that's all." I tried to sound convincing
but I guess I still had half a mind to forget my
promise to June. That trip was something I really
wanted to do.

I had spent two days thinking about what to
do. I hated not going with Pete but on the other
hand that room of my own was important, too.
Besides, I had really promised June first.

"What's this important thing you gotta do?" Pete's mouth was all screwed up like he wanted to spit instead of talk. The scarf around his neck seemed to be mad too because just then a wind came along and the long dangling end came around and smacked me right on the back of the head.

At least that took the mean look off Pete's face for a minute.

"Listen Pete, in a couple of months we'll get the whole summer to do what we want. We'll be able to take a week or more for a ride to the Cape. It'll be warmer weather then, too, and make for a better ride." I was thinking fast because I didn't want to have a real blowout with Pete. He was my best friend. And, in my way, I really loved the guy, rotten quirks and all.

"Yeah, but then we won't have anyone to go with and your mother will put up a stink. Come on, Scott, this is it, don't frig it up."

Pete didn't tell me anything I hadn't thought of myself the night before. But I wasn't going to agree with him.

"Naw, Pete, by this summer I'll be able to do and go anywhere I want without my old lady's permission. She knows I'm not a kid anymore . . ." but I didn't get a chance to elaborate.

"It's that damned June, isn't it?" Pete burst out with it like he had just discovered the last piece to a puzzle. He had stopped walking and was standing there in front of me, blocking my way.

"That's what it is, isn't it?"

I nodded my head because there didn't seem much point to saying anything.

"Shit, I knew this would happen. Girls. They ruin everything. They're nothing but trouble."

"Come on, Pete, you know you wouldn't say that if you had a girl of your own." I knew I shouldn't have said it the minute it came out of my mouth. Talking about Pete's problems with girls was just like hitting him in the balls. It really zapped him.

"Girls are good for only one thing"—Pete punctuated his opinion by poking me hard in the belly with his free fist—"screwing!"

I knew Pete would never start to fight me unless he was crazy mad. He always played it safe and made sure that someone else was around to do his fighting for him. He knew I could beat the shit out of him.

"Look Pete, there's no point in getting sore at me. It won't change anything. After all, I can't help it if a guy has to take care of his girl first." I was feeling lousy and good at the same time. Lousy because I could understand Pete feeling hurt. If I didn't have June I would've felt the same way about anybody giving up a terrific trip just for a girl. But there was June and now I was feeling rotten because I was hurting Pete. But then again I felt kind of superior, like I had something he didn't. It was the first time I could ever remember feeling that way with Pete.

Usually it was the other way around. But now I was feeling special and it was a good feeling. It kept me from getting steamed up over Pete's acting like such an ass about the whole thing.

"Why do you have to back down on our trip? Why don't you tell June you've got something else to do?" We had started walking again. I kept my eyes on the ground in front of me so I wouldn't have to look at the pained expression on Pete's face.

How could I explain to Pete I liked him a hell of a lot but being with him wasn't the same as being with June? He acted like it was a contest or something between them. There just wasn't any choice.

"Ah Pete, you can still go on the trip. You aren't stuck. Why don't you call up one of the other guys?"

"Christ, Scott, since you started going with that broad you haven't been any fun at all."

"She's no broad."

I knew I shouldn't have said it. Damned creep. Now he would know how to reach me.

"Sure she is. I bet she gives out with everybody." Pete had a tight grin on his face. His teeth were sharp and pointy, and when he drew up his lips real tight, he could've passed for a sneering rat. I could feel myself getting pissed off and I tried to stop listening to him. He was a foul-mouthed bastard when he got mad enough.

I didn't care what he called me. After all we had plenty of fights before and I got in my share of words. But this time it was different. When he bad-mouthed June, I had to struggle with myself not to break his neck. I tried not to listen to him, to block him out with my words.

"Look Pete," I said, closing his mouth before he said something I couldn't help but hit him for, "I know you're sore and I don't blame you . . ."

"Thanks a lot." He sounded disgusted.

" . . . but honest to God," I pleaded, "I did promise to be with June before I talked with you about the trip. I swear it!" I was holding his arm, making him stand still and listen to me. I didn't want him to turn me off like I knew he would if he got sore enough.

"I understand, all right. I understand that from now on I come second." Pete's voice came out kind of queer, like he was holding his throat tight together to keep from crying.

"Ah, Pete, it's not that way at all. It's just that I really like her a lot. And hell," I let go of his arm and gave him a short light clip on his jaw, "you just can't kiss as good as a girl."

"Yeah, but I still think you're a jerk. She pushes you around and makes you do whatever she wants." I could see he was still itching to get into a real battle. But I kept myself from fighting with him even though by this time I figured he deserved it.

What a joker he was, too. He called June bossy. He was the worst damn boss in the world when he wanted something. He did anything he could to get his way. I wanted to say something about it to him, like how he sure didn't see himself if he thought June was bossy. But there wasn't much point in telling him anything. It wouldn't have done any good. Besides, we were just about at his house and I wanted to beat it away from his big mouth and go home.

"Listen, I'll talk to you later," I said, trying to make a fast getaway. But Pete's face stopped me long enough to hear him finish. He had a kind of lonesome, hurt look. *Like a scared, lost, little kid,* I thought, feeling awful sorry for him. *If only I could fix him up with someone.*

I had tried that but June said none of her friends would date him because he had a reputation for being a creep.

"Well, I guess if you're gonna stick with her . . . there's nothing I can do." The expression on his face made a sudden change back to the good old Pete I remembered. "But you'll see I'm right. Girls do stink. You'll see." *He always has to have the last word,* I kind of laughed to myself, glad that he didn't look so down anymore.

"Ah, Pete, honest, that's not so. You ought to try and get to know her. She's really a good kid."

Pete turned to go up his steps. He stopped on his porch and turned around and looked down at me.

"Yeah, I'll bet . . ." His voice was so low I had to read his lips.

"I'll get in touch with you later." I smiled at

him, waved my hand in a semi-salute, and went home feeling like I had just been through a war. I was beat, but I thought I had won.

"Scott, what's all the hammering for?" My mother hadn't been around long enough to discuss building the room so I had gone ahead and started without bothering to tell her about it. I had just come up from the basement after laying down some of the two-by-fours I had found there.

"I'm building a room downstairs," I figured I better tell her right off and get it over with.

"A room? What for?" She had a surprised look on her face like she never heard of a guy needing a place to call his own.

"Listen, ma, Dave's gonna stick around here for the next couple of years, right?" She nodded her head, still looking at me like my head was screwed on lopsided or something. I went on. "Well, I need a place of my own. With Dave and Lisa around all the time there's no privacy anywhere in this house. I can't have my friends over without somebody around here always butting into my business."

"I'm sorry, Scott, but I don't think it's safe in the basement. There's no air and besides what will you do when we get another flood down there?"

I saw the whole spiel coming. I went right on talking to stop her from saying anything more. "All my friends have their own room." I should have known better than to use that argument. It never worked with her and it wasn't going to now.

"That doesn't concern me. If all your friends turned their hair green, would that mean that you would have to do the same thing? We're discussing you, Scott, my son. You're the one I care about."

She was standing with her back leaning against the stove, her arms crossed in front of her chest. Her face had that "no way" expression on it.

"God dammit, I don't understand you. You don't give a damn about us because you're too busy running around doing whatever you want. But the second I ask for something you put the whammy on it." My voice was growing louder and I was beginning to get burned up.

"Scott, you're not living down in the basement. And I don't like what you are saying to me."

"All right, but just tell me why. Why can't I live down there? I can dig dry wells around the foundation to stop the floods. Besides, I plan on getting indoor-outdoor carpeting so the water won't hurt it." There, I thought, satisfied she couldn't answer that.

"And what happens if it does flood and you step in the water and turn on a light switch? Don't you realize you can get killed that way?"

She was so damn smart. Arguing with her

was like fighting with twenty of my smartest friends and then some.

I sat down at the table feeling like the world's biggest loser. What was I going to do now? But I was mad. Why should everyone but me have it the way he wanted it?

"I've gotta have my own room. I gotta have a place where I can shut the door and not have people buggin' me all the time." My voice sounded awful high in my ears. It seemed I always ended up feeling like a little kid when I argued with her. It was like fighting a solid block of stone. I'd try to crack her but she never moved or changed. I ended up feeling whipped, sore, and down.

"All right, Scott." She undid her arms and came over to sit at the table with me. It was funny how she would change so suddenly. She made me dizzy. I'd be sorer than hell at her and then out of nowhere she'd stop hollering and start to make sense. She said the reason we always fought was because we were too much alike. Sometimes I wondered if I'd ever be able to win an argument with her.

"Look ma," I said, looking at her steady, trying to talk real calm and cool, "whenever I have my friends over, Dave is in there shutting us up. Lisa's always listening in or butting in telling the guys things about me. That really burns me up."

"You mean she embarrasses you?"

"Yeah. You wouldn't believe some of the

things she tells people about me." I was sore just thinking about that blabber-mouthed brat.

"I'll talk with her about it."

"Yeah, but I still need a place of my own. Some place where I can be alone." I saw I was making some headway.

"Yes . . . but I really don't want you sleeping down there. Besides the danger, there's no bathroom."

"I'll use the sink in the basement."

"Not to pee in, you won't."

I started to chuckle at that. She thought it was pretty funny too because her eyes crinkled up and she smiled at me.

Suddenly, I realized how long it had been since we talked like friends. *Jeez,* I thought, *it's been a long time since we smiled together.* It felt pretty good, too.

"What if I don't sleep there?" It had hit me, just like that. After all, I just wanted some place to have when my friends were over. I didn't have to sleep there, too.

She looked interested, like maybe I had finally come up with a good idea. I kept talking.

"Yeah, I can still sleep upstairs, but I can fix up downstairs just for having my friends over, like for a party or something." I was thinking out loud now and getting pretty excited. It was a great idea and I could do it. I knew I could because I could see my mother wasn't jumping in to say no right away.

"I could still fix it up and stuff like that. Get some kind of sofa down there . . ."

"Wait a minute, Scott. This sounds like it might be pretty expensive to do."

"Naw, I can get the furniture second-hand. All the guys have old junk in their attics I could use. All I'm going to need is some plywood and paneling and wiring for the lighting." I could see now it was going to be an easy job after all.

"That's an awful lot of work. Besides, what do you know about wiring? If you don't do it right, the whole house will go up in flames." Her voice told me she was beginning to get shaky on the idea.

"Don't worry about the wiring," I rushed in to say before she changed her mind again, "Pete's brother-in-law-to-be is an electrician and he'll help me. Anyhow, it's not that tough to do. We did plenty of wiring and stuff in shop last year."

"But what do you know about building rooms? I have a feeling you're going to end up spending a fortune and have a disaster on your hands."

"Listen ma, I already put up the skeleton. It's working out just fine."

"What did you use for wood?"

"The two-by-fours we had in the basement."

"Do you know how much they cost?"

I could see what was coming next so I jumped right in.

"I'll pay you for them."

"That's not the point. You should have asked permission first before you used them."

"How could I? You're too busy running around with your jerky boyfriends to be like other mothers who stay at home."

She didn't like that. She got up from the table and walked over to the sink and let the water run into it. The sound of the water was all I could hear besides the motor on the refrigerator which made such a racket that when it finally stopped, the house sounded like it had died.

"Scott, you can build your room downstairs."

Her voice was clear and quiet. She said every word so I couldn't miss anything. She was madder than I had ever seen her. Not mad like she was going to beat me up mad. But mad like I knew there was nothing but blue-white flame inside her.

She went on, "However, I expect you to pay for everything yourself. I hold you completely responsible for anything you do in the basement. Is that understood?"

I stood up wishing she would hit me instead of just standing there letting the water run over her hands, her back to me. I felt rotten.

I went upstairs wondering if I would ever do anything that would please her. No matter how hard I tried nothing seemed to be right. I passed algebra with a B and she told me I should've gotten an A. When I got my job, she made a stink because she didn't like the idea of my borrowing her car to get to work.

Now I had to figure out how I was going to get the money to pay for the stuff I would need to build the room. I was going to get it done no matter what. It was going to be the best-looking room she ever saw.

Dave was at work so I sat down on my bed and turned up my radio as loud as I could. The bass sounds bounced off the walls of the room and I sat back with my head resting against the wall thinking about what stuff I would have to clear out of the basement to make the space I wanted for my room. I didn't care if my mother was sore at me. It didn't matter because once she said I could go ahead and build the room she wouldn't back down no matter what. If she said so, she'd keep her word. That was one good thing about her. But that was the only good thing I could think of about her right then.

Pretty soon I'd have my own place where I could close the door and not have to let anybody in. All I needed was enough plywood and paneling to get started and a way of getting the stuff into the house. I went into my mother's room and got out the telephone book and started calling places that sold lumber.

"How much?" I wrote down the amount on the pad I had found on my mother's night table. "That's the cheapest cut I can use, huh? Okay, thank you very much."

I hung up the phone and looked at the figures on the pad. How was I going to get that kind of money? Then I figured out what to do.

"Is this Allstone Lumber Company? Do you deliver?" They did, but they charged extra for the service. That didn't matter to me though. I wasn't planning on paying for it for a while anyhow.

"You charge, don't you? " I tried to sound like I thought my old man would have sounded.

"Yes sir," the guy on the other end of the phone said.

After I placed the order I hung up the phone and sat there on my mother's bed grinning to myself. Because I was able to charge the lumber and other stuff I ordered, I'd have a whole month to get the money together. By that time I'd have the room built and the money earned. That was the easy part. I'd just get my boss to give me more work hours.

When the back of my head started to work later on I remembered my boss said business was slow and he might just have to let one of us guys go . . . *It couldn't be me,* I thought, remembering quickly how he was always telling me how great my work was.

The wood, nails, and the rest of the supplies I ordered were coming the next day. For a second I wondered if I ought to ask my boss about my job before I let the lumber company make the delivery.

What the hell, I don't care, I'm gonna do it

no matter what happens. And I don't care what I have to do to get it. After all, something had to go right for me sometime, I reasoned. But I went back down to the basement with a creepy feeling in the pit of my stomach. Like there was something I forgot about that was going to make me trouble. The rest of the night I worked getting things ready to throw away and make room for the lumber I had ordered.

Earlier, at dinner, I mentioned the lumber was going to be delivered the next day.

"C.O.D.?" my mother asked.

"No, I charged it."

She picked up some food with her fork and looked at it, then at me. Finally she said, "You realize, of course, that if you don't pay your bills I will be held responsible for them?"

"Look ma, I told you, don't worry, it's all taken care of." She gave me a look that said she wanted to say something else to me. But instead, she just took a deep breath and started eating.

It was past midnight when I finally got too tired to work anymore. So I went up to bed feeling good about all the work I had done that night. I was beat enough to fall asleep without thinking about anything. The last I remember was a color picture of the room all finished and me and June sitting on this gorgeous big sofa nice and close together . . .

*I*t was finished! I watched June as she pushed the curtains on the windows into place, closing out the morning light in the room. She had to stretch up real high to reach the top of the curtain. Her body looked like a ballet dancer or something, all graceful and slim.

She's a great-looking chick, I thought, feeling good she was my girl. There were plenty of guys who would've liked to have us break up so they could get to date her. Sometimes thinking about that kind of scared me. She was so terrific, I wondered why she wanted me. But most of the time I didn't think about it and that was better.

"How do they look, Scott?" June had picked out the material and made the curtains herself. I knew she wanted me to compliment her about the perfect job she had done on them.

"They look terrific, really great." I came up behind her and put my arms around her waist, hugging her close to me, and gave her a kiss on her ear lobe. *Jeez, she feels good,* I thought pulling her as close to me as I could.

She giggled and kind of wiggled a little bit, and stretched herself out against me like a kitten does when you pet it and it wants more. I could feel myself beginning to float into outer space and wow, it felt wild.

"What should we do to celebrate?" June's question brought me back down to the basement floor fast. It's funny about things like that. If a guy begins to fly and the girl doesn't . . . well it kind of lets him drop like a slack wind can do to a flying kite. I mean, it grounds a guy . . . bam . . . a real fast dive into a cold pool.

"I guess we should do something." I could've thought of the something to do, but that last drop to the ground made me keep my mouth shut.

June and I had talked about sex and how we felt about making out and stuff like that. She really wasn't a tease or anything like that, but I guess I learned from her that girls just aren't like guys. It takes them a lot longer to get to the same place a guy gets to when he kisses his girl or even sees a good-looking broad.

"I know what we can do!" June had a one-track mind sometimes, I thought, feeling kind of sore at her. It was funny about that, too. I could never figure out why I felt that way. I would be flying one minute and then down and sore the next. Man, those hormones can really drive a guy up a wall.

"Let's have a picnic," she said, turning around to face me. I didn't want to let her go.

"Today?" I asked.

"Of course, silly," she said, kissing me lightly on my chin. "We can bring down a blanket to cover up the carpet, and the radio from your room . . ."

"Yeah, that's a great idea," I said, excited now that I understood what and where she wanted to picnic. It sounded terrific.

"We can really test out the room," I said, meaning we could lock the door and have privacy, no people popping in on us when we didn't want them.

"Let's go get the stuff we'll need now from your room. We can make the food up and bring it down here after we're all set, okay?"

The two of us were grinning like mad when we got up to the kitchen. My mother was sitting at the kitchen table reading her paper and drinking her cup of tea. She looked up at us as we came into the room. She smiled at June and said hello. Then she looked back down at her paper.

"Hey ma, you ought to go down and look at the room. It's finished."

Ever since she had to pay the bill from the lumber company she had been sore as hell at me. I guess it was stupid not to have made certain about getting the money before I charged the stuff. But I really figured I would have it all by the time the bill came in. I didn't figure on any problem. Who could have known my boss would cut back my working hours so I was only earning half of what I was getting when I ordered the wood?

My mother and I finally ended up making a deal where I gave her something every week until I paid the whole thing off. But she was still sore at me. She hadn't looked down in the basement once since I started working on it.

"Go ahead, ma, take a look, willya?" I was really pleading. I wanted her to see what I had done. I wanted her to say it was terrific and I wasn't such a low cruddy creep after all. I hated it when she was mad at me . . . it made me feel all tight and sick inside. It was a rotten feeling to have. Sometimes I wondered if anybody ever gets over wanting his folks to like them . . .

"In a minute, Scott." She looked at me and then stood up. "All right, let's see what you've done."

Well, you could've knocked me over with a look just then. I never figured she would really listen to me. Jeez, it really made a guy wonder about things, like how tough it was to figure people out.

I walked down the steps in front of her. June decided to go up to my room and collect the things we'd need for our picnic. She must've realized this was a good time to make herself scarce. She knew all about how sore my mother was and how I felt about it. That was another terrific thing about having a girlfriend I could really talk to. I could really get inside myself and let it all hang out and not have to worry about her teasing me like Pete would've done. He would never have been able to resist throwing some of the things I told June back at me at some time or other, just to get even for something or other.

My mother followed me down into the basement. I opened the door to my newly finished room and flipped on the light switch. Se stood behind me, so quiet I could almost hear her thinking. I tried to look around the room like I had never seen it before. I wanted to see it the way I figured she would be looking at it.

I looked at the wood-paneled walls. The hardest thing about putting them up was taking perfect measurements. They were awful expensive and I didn't want to mess any of them up. Then I looked up at the ceiling. Dave and Pete had helped me to put it up. That was a tough job, too. I almost killed myself trying to do it alone. June was just too little to help even though she really tried hard. She was a great help painting and puttying and she even helped with the measuring and cutting. But the ceiling tiles were heavy and hard to handle, even for me . . .

"It looks very good, Scott." She sounded like she really meant it and I could feel the air filling out my lungs. I must've been holding my breath without realizing it, waiting for her to say something.

"What did you finally do about putting in your electrical wiring?" She switched the wall light on and off a couple of times. Then she went over to an old lamp I had recovered and repaired. I rescued it from the mess of junk I had tossed out from the basement. She turned on the light, looking surprised but pleased when it worked.

"I did it myself. I had some help from my shop teacher at school . . . laying out plans for the wiring and figuring out the amount of voltage I'd need . . . stuff like that. I did the actual work myself, though." I was feeling pretty proud of my work just then and wanted her to understand . . .

"Hmm, you did a good job," she smiled at me. "You're sure it's safe." But she said it like she was sure it was. There wasn't any question in her voice.

"Yeah, absolutely perfect. I used two different lines so I wouldn't ever overload." I was beginning to warm up to the subject. I wanted to tell her how hard I had worked. "One of the toughest parts of the job was making the right calculations for the wall switches and the warps in the ceiling and floor."

She walked over to the corner of the room and ran her hand over the place where the two walls met.

"Very neat." That was a real compliment

coming from my old lady. She wasn't like most mothers. Since my dad left she had taken over most of the carpentry in the house. In fact, she was a pretty decent plumber, too.

"You've done a good job here, Scott. And what's more important to me, you've finished it." She looked at me and I felt relieved to see she wasn't sore anymore. It made me feel good to hear her say something nice to me for a change.

We stood there quietly for a minute kind of studying each other.

"I've been in touch with your math teacher, Scott. He tells me you've really made quite an improvement in his class. That's good." She started toward the door and then turned back to face me. "I think . . . perhaps, you are becoming the man you should be after all, hmm, Scott?"

She left me standing there in the middle of the room feeling like someone had gone over me with an electric shock. My whole body felt tingling and alive. I was so proud of myself . . . I felt great. She really liked it. I had done it and she liked it. The smile on her face had lit me up. It was like the times when I was a little kid and would bring her a flower I picked on my way home from school. After I gave it to her she would hug and kiss me and thank me for being me. I could have lifted up the house just then.

"And then what did she say?" June and I were sitting on the floor of our new room, my blue bed quilt under us and a tray she had found in the kitchen on the floor in front of us filled with sandwiches, fruit, and sodas. I had brought down a couple of pillows, too, so that after we ate lunch we could lie back and listen to some music over the radio.

We sat close together, our shoulders almost touching.

I swallowed what was in my mouth and told June what my mother had said and how terrific I felt about it.

"That's great for you, Scott. I'm awfully glad she isn't mad at you anymore."

"Me too. And that's really funny, you know? Like why should I care what she thinks?" I looked at June, wondering if she knew the answer. She nodded her head.

"I feel that way about my mother, too. And you know what I think about her." June's mother was square with a capital S. She was so out of touch with the real world that it was impossible to find anything at all to talk to her about.

June's father . . . he was another one. He lived in the house although it was hard to tell if he was around most of the time. He never made any waves. He left it all to June's nutty mother.

It was a crazy family. June couldn't figure out why her parents stayed married. They acted like they hated each other most of the time they were together. From some of the stories she told me it sounded like my house used to when my parents were married to each other and living together. And I could remember how awful it was then.

I was feeling full of food and happy all over. It had been a pretty terrific day so far and with June next to me and a lock on the door I began to think about how much greater the day could be if . . .

I got up and went over to turn on the radio. We had one really good station that played the best sounding records. Some of the other DJ's just stuck anything on the table and they didn't care about the sound. But this guy loved to play stuff that would blow my mind. I loved to lie in my bed late at night and fall asleep with the earplug in my ear and the warm sound rocking me to sleep.

I took the tray off the blanket so we could stretch out on the floor without dumping everything. Then I turned out the light and June and I lay on the soft quilt over the carpet, our pillows close together, our bodies folded into each other, my arms wrapped around her, listening to the sound. It was all so good I felt like crying. Crazy. I swallowed hard. I kissed her mouth and she kissed me back.

I always wondered what it would be like to make love. It wasn't like anything I ever read about.

After it was over we held each other close and kissed until the feeling that had caught us up and stopped the world from turning melted away, leaving us lying there on the floor in the darkened room all warm and happy.

"I love you," I told her again, meaning it more than ever.

We talked for a while about how we felt and then June let out a giggle.

"My mother would die if she saw me now."

"I guess she would." And then I thought a little. "Hey, that's not why you did it . . . to get even with your mother, was it?" It wasn't a pretty thought, but I could understand her feeling that way.

"No . . . at least, I don't think so . . . well, maybe a little . . . I love you, Scott." She rolled over to me and kissed me. Then she took her finger and ran it lightly over my face past my mouth. I kissed it as it passed by and thought I didn't really care what her reasons were. It was okay with me.

"Jeez." A thought just tumbled into my head, like a ball coming from nowhere and then suddenly it was in my hand. "Do you think my old lady does this with those guys she dates?" I felt sick for a minute, thinking about it.

"So, what if she does?" And June sounded like she didn't think too much of my not liking the idea.

"I don't know, it just doesn't seem right." I thought about all the creeps I had seen around my house since my dad left. There wasn't any of them I liked. Most of them would either ignore me or make too much noise about me. Usually

I'd disappear from sight when I saw one of them coming.

"I guess even your mother has to have somebody her age to be friends with," June said slowly, like she was thinking hard to say the right thing to me.

"She's got plenty of girlfriends," I said, feeling stupid about lying there so close and happy with June and bitching about my mother dating guys.

June was running her finger around my body, outlining me like I was being traced on a piece of paper. It felt nice.

"Would you rather be with Pete right now?" she giggled, knowing damn well what the answer was. So I grabbed her and we wrestled a little bit, tickling each other. It sure beat fighting with any guy I knew. I kissed her on the tip of her cute little nose.

"You're right, you don't feel like Pete," I said, giving her a pinch on her backside. "You're softer."

"Thank you." She giggled again. "But you didn't answer my question."

"Yeah, I know. My mother would rather be with guys than her girlfriends. It's just that they're all such creeps." But no matter what I said I still didn't like the idea of my mother making out with one of those guys.

Then a really horrible thought hit me.

"Jeez, June, what if she decided to marry one of those jerks and he became my stepfather?" The pain in my head told me I was scared as hell of such a thing happening. One of those creeps for a father. Even June's kisses and sweet words couldn't make the awful feeling I had go away . . .

*I*t had been one rotten evening; one of the worst times in my life. I knew it was going to stink even before it started but there wasn't much I could have done to stop it. Not that I didn't try.

"Scott," my mother greeted me when I got back from work, "we're all going out to dinner tonight."

"Naw," I told her, "I'm bushed. One of the other dishwashers didn't show up so I had to work a double shift."

"I'm sorry about that," she said, like it didn't really matter how hard I sweated for a buck, "but I want you to meet someone tonight. It's very important."

"Jeez, ma, not tonight. Maybe some other

time, huh?" I wasn't in the mood to be polite to anybody and I wasn't even going to try. I started to leave the room so I could get up to my bed and lie down, but . . .

"Scott, you have no choice. Get washed and dressed. I want you ready in half an hour." And her voice made me believe she meant it.

"Who's so important, anyhow?" I figured it must be some long lost relative or something. Why else would she have been in such a sweat?

"It's a man I've been dating . . . I want to have you meet him . . ."

"Listen, ma, I'm not interested in your boyfriends. I don't want to meet him. All I want to do is lie down." I started up the steps to my room.

"Scott," her voice stopped me before I got to the second step.

"Ma, come on, willya? Some other time."

She came to the bottom of the stairs and looked up at me. "I'm thinking about marrying him. I think it would be a good idea for you to come along tonight." Her voice was cold. It was like a sharp knife had just punctured my gut. I felt the cold shoot through my body leaving me standing on the step frozen, not able to run away and not able to get up the energy to argue. She didn't give me a chance to say anything. Anyway, what was there to say? So I just stood there and listened to her going on . . .

"I've been working all day, too. I know that you're tired. But you had better come along."

By the time she finished convincing me I had to go with them my head was beginning to work again. I was getting curious about this guy she wanted me to meet so much.

"Did I ever see him around the house?" I hoped not because there wasn't anyone I ever saw hanging around I would have wanted to see again.

"No, that's just it. It seems every time I've been with him, you've been out working or dating or something else." She put her hand over mine where I had it resting on the staircase railing and the way she looked at me I knew I was sunk. It was in the bag. I couldn't disappoint her when she gave me that mother-love treatment. If I did, it would have made me feel guilty as all hell.

"Okay, I'll go," I finally gave in, "but let's not make it all night long, okay?" She nodded, smiling, and I moved my feet up to the top of the steps. They felt like I had ten-ton hiking boots on them by the time I got all the way up.

Well, we all went. Lisa, Dave, and me. We sat at the table staring at this guy and watching my mother act like a jackass, giggling and blinking her eyelashes at him. I looked at Dave a couple of times to see if I could tell what he was thinking. But, like usual, he was deadpanned. Lisa ate the whole thing up. I wasn't too surprised about that because she spent all her time reading romantic crap. The kind of books where the boy wants the girl, and the girl wants the boy, and finally they get together and make out . . . She reads stuff like that for hours. So I didn't pay too much attention to her sitting there lapping it all up like it was so much chocolate ice cream.

The guy asked us some stupid questions but I managed not to talk too much. Dave mumbled some and Lisa . . . well, she loved to talk.

My mother must've got the hint we weren't having such a hot time because right after dessert she said, "Well, the boys have to get up early to get to work tomorrow, so I think we'd better get on home." Now she knew Sunday we didn't have to get up early, so I knew she was reading our signals right. Sometimes my old lady could be pretty sharp. Anyway it was one hell of a relief to get out of the restaurant and put an end to our misery.

The three of us beat it upstairs as soon as we got in the door, hollering thanks for dinner and stuff like that on our way upstairs.

"Isn't he cute?" Lisa started gushing as soon as we got into our room and closed the door. Dave just went over to his desk and fiddled with some stuff on it.

"What do you think, Dave?" I wasn't going to answer Lisa's question. It was too dumb.

"He's okay, I guess." But the way he said it I knew he was thinking otherwise.

"I think he's a jerk. Did you see the way he paid the bill, like every buck he handed out he had to tear out a finger from his hand. He's a creep." I didn't like him the minute I met him and the feeling grew when I saw how he acted with my mother. He treated her like she was a little kid and she let him do it.

"He's got a nice beard." Lisa wasn't dumb, but she was doing an awful good imitation.

"Shut up, Lisa. Do you want that jerk for a stepfather?" I wanted to make her disappear, but there was no way. She wasn't going into her room until she had a chance to talk.

"Stepfather?" She looked surprised, like she really didn't think about that happening.

"Yeah, stupid. Why do you think ma wanted all of us to go out with them tonight?" Maybe Lisa just needed to know what was going on because after she realized what I was telling her, her tune changed fast.

"I don't want him for a stepfather, eyuk." She made like she wanted to puke.

"Yeah, that's more like it. You go shooting your mouth off to ma about how great and cute this jerk is and the next thing you know we'll be living with him, permanently."

Dave didn't say anything all the time Lisa and I were talking but I could see he was listening.

"Dave, when ma asks us what we think about him you better be the one to tell her. She'll listen to you. If we tell her, she'll just say we don't know anything or shit like that." I meant what I told him, too. Dave was like a grown-up to ma. She would talk to him about money and her troubles and listen to him when he would tell her what to do. If Dave said we all didn't like the guy, she'd listen. But it had to come from Dave. If I told her she'd just say I was hysterical or scared and try to psych me out of it and we'd probably end up screaming at each other.

"Will you do it, Dave?" Lisa asked him. Her face had a worried look on it like she finally understood how serious the whole thing was. After all she didn't want any strange creep walking into her life and messing around anymore than I did. That is once she understood what it was all about.

Dave didn't talk, just nodded his head. We could see he was thinking hard. Dave wouldn't shoot off his mouth. Maybe that's why ma listened to him.

Anyhow, when we finally got to bed and Lisa wasn't there to bug me I called out in the dark to him.

"Dave, whatdya really think about him? Do you think I'm right?" I needed him to tell me because if he agreed then everything would be okay.

"Yeah, I guess so," he answered me, his voice soft and quiet like the shadows on the wall.

I fell asleep feeling pretty good. Dave would take care of everything.

The next morning I opened my eyes, looked at the clock, and thought to myself it was great it was Sunday and I could sleep until noon if I wanted. Then I heard my mother calling us from her bedroom.

Lisa opened the door to our room and popped in her head. "Hey, you guys, ma wants you."

My stomach took a double take. This is it. I knew it. I looked over at Dave who still looked more than half asleep.

"This is it, Dave," I said, kind of whispering so that no one but him would hear me. "It's up to you, Dave, okay?" He nodded, but my heart stayed in my mouth anyway.

"Okay, kids, what did you think of him?" Just like that. We barely had gotten settled into our spots on her bed when she came out with it. I looked over at Dave and out of the corner of my eye I could see Lisa doing the same thing. Of course, ma caught on real quick so she looked at Dave, too.

"Well, Dave," she said. "It looks as though you're the spokesman for the crowd . . . let's hear it."

"Well . . . we really don't know him very well . . ."

I could see Dave was going to cop out on us. Him and his logic.

"Ma, you're not really gonna marry that creep are you?" I had to say something. If I let Dave go on it might have ended up with her believing we thought he was okay or something else just as bad.

"Well, he's asked me. I haven't said yes, yet." She didn't look too happy seeing how none of us were overjoyed with her news. The three of us just stared at her. I guess we were all feeling pretty scared. I knew I was.

"Ma, he's awful old." Lisa popped up. Boy, she could really be okay when she wanted to.

"Yeah, and besides I didn't like the way he talked to you, bossing you around and stuff," I said.

Finally Dave got into the act.

"Ma, we really didn't like him very much. But . . . it's your life and you're the one who should . . . well, who must make the decision, not us."

Dave, the saint. I was really sore at myself for trusting him.

"Shut up Dave," I shouted. "Maybe you don't care because you're able to leave and go live at college if things get lousy around here. But Lisa and me . . . we're stuck. We'd have to live with that guy." I balled my hand tightly; my fingernails cut into my palms. I was ready to shove my fist right into his big mouth.

"That's true, Scott," my mother said just as I was ready to pull the punch. "But in a very few years you'll be leaving here, too."

"And then I'm gonna leave, too," Lisa said, sticking her tongue out at me.

"So what has that got to do with anything?" I said, disgusted with the way the discussion was going.

"Well, do you plan to stay here with me and keep me company for the rest of my life?" ma asked, looking straight at me.

"Don't be ridiculous. Not me. I'm getting out as soon as I'm eighteen." *And she better believe it,* I added to myself.

"That's just what I'm talking about, Scott. If I don't have someone of my own to be with, like you and June . . ."

"But that's different . . ."

"No, Scott, it's not different. I'm no different from you. I need someone of my own, too." And the way she said it made me remember some of the things June and I talked about the times we were together. We both had decided that life was much more fun when everything was shared with someone else. It wasn't much fun doing things alone . . .

"Mom, are you gonna marry him?" Lisa had one good thing about her. She always asked the right questions. At least she always kept asking until she got an answer. She never got sidetracked like me.

"Well, actually, the reason I wanted you to go out with us last night was because I wasn't certain whether I was making a fair judgment."

"What does that mean?" Lisa said, beating me to it.

"I guess it means I really didn't like him too much either. But I needed the three of you, and your clear eyes," she said, looking at each one of us, "to help me make my decision." She smiled at us and made a sound like she was sighing with relief.

"So you're not gonna marry him?" Lisa sure could clear up a subject. I decided that maybe I should tell her to get on the school newspaper. *She would probably make a terrific reporter,* I thought to myself.

"No, I'm not going to marry him. But . . ."

We all looked up at her.

"Probably, someday, I will meet someone I will want to marry. Then, if I think it's the right thing, as Dave said, I'm the one who will have to make the final decision about my life." She took time out for a breath. "But I promise you this, that whatever I do, if it's good for me, it'll be good for all of you."

I pulled myself off the bed feeling a hell of a lot better.

"I figured you were too smart to go for that jerk," I said.

"You did, did you? So how come you had such a worried expression on your face when you first came in here this morning?"

There was no point telling her how maybe I had a tiny doubt in my mind, so I just grinned.

"You making breakfast this morning?" I asked. It was time to change the subject.

"No, Scott. You're making your own breakfast. Just make certain you clean up after yourself."

I left the three of them and went down to the kitchen. I telephoned June and told her about the lousy evening with my mother's boy-friend and how it turned out all right for me in the end.

"Anyhow," I told June, "even if my mother did find some guy, she wouldn't marry him if we really hated him."

"I bet she would, if she were really in love with him," June answered, making me worried all over again. She would know about how women act better than I would, I supposed. But I didn't like thinking or talking about it. After all it worked out all right this time . . .

It wasn't until some time later that I really understood what Dave and my mother and June were really saying to me. When I finally realized what they meant, I guess it was just about the most important thing that ever happened to me in my whole life, and the best.

I was looking out my bedroom window and watching the sun light up the leaves in the big tree on our lawn into different shades of green. Dave and I used to have fun when we were little kids trying to count all the different shades of the same color we could see in our yard. I remember the first time I looked at the grass and saw it really wasn't all the same color like I always thought. After all, green was green, wasn't it? But it wasn't. It was green that looked like blue or yellow or brown, but somehow they all looked green. I was thinking about how life was something like that, all shaded instead of one solid color, when I heard the phone ring. It's funny how noises can take my thoughts right out of my head. But once the phone rang all I did was to listen hard to find out if it was for me.

"Scott, Pete's on the phone," my mother called up to me from downstairs.

I took it on her bedroom phone.

"Guess what?" Pete was playing guessing games again. But like always I played along with him, at least until I got sick and tired and threatened to hang up if he didn't give out.

"What?"

"Keith's old man came through with a car for Keith's birthday." Pete sounded all excited like he was the one who had gotten the car. We were all in Driver Ed. that term so I knew it wouldn't be too long before Pete got a car, too. I knew I wasn't going to get one because my mother said I could have one when I could buy it for myself. I knew what that meant . . .

"Isn't that great? I mean his old man coming up with a brand-new car." Pete was really impressed. That was something too, because it took a hell of a lot to reach Pete.

"So what's the big deal?" I couldn't figure out what all the excitement was about. Other guys we knew had cars. What was such a big deal about Keith's?

"Didn't I tell you the story? Boy, that Keith, he sure is something else." Pete was beginning to drive me up the wall.

"You gonna tell me or do I have to stand here all day?"

"Remember the time when Keith ran away from home to get away from his old lady?"

How could I forget that. Jeez, the cops called my mother to find out if I knew where he went. After what Pete told me about Keith's mother I couldn't blame him for running. What I couldn't figure out was why he came back and stayed. His old lady was a real bitch to live with. She hated Keith, at least Keith thought so and told that to Pete . . .

"Yeah, so what? That was last year . . ." According to the story Pete told me, Keith had headed straight for his old man's place in the woods where they used to go hunting and fishing together. I guess that was the one place that Keith really felt happy. Anyhow, it was his old man who found him there after Keith had been gone a couple of weeks . . .

"Well, I just found out from him why he came back home and stayed . . ."

I was no great pal of Keith's, but after hearing about him I always felt a little sorry for him. He certainly got a rotten deal when his parents divorced.

"Scott, it's wild." Pete laughed his low, deep belly laugh over the phone and sounded real broken up.

"Stop clowning around and tell me, willya?" Damned if Pete didn't always get to me.

"It was a bribe," Pete shouted over the phone at me.

"A bribe? What for?"

"So that the old man didn't have to take him."

"Jeez," I breathed out slowly, taking time to think about what Pete just told me. "You mean his old man didn't want Keith to live with him so bad that he was willing to get stuck for the price of a new car rather than . . ." *Jeez . . . that really shits.* "I suppose part of the deal was his staying put at his mother's?" I asked Pete.

"Yeah, they didn't want any repeat action. You know, if he wouldn't be a pain in the neck then . . ."

I thought about Keith and how he must have felt about making such a deal with his dad. No wonder Keith was such a nut . . . with parents like his . . . Jeez . . .

"You wantta go for a ride?" Pete asked.

"I have a date to bike up to the reservoir with June today." My head was still filled with the story Pete just told me. I knew there were plenty of rotten parents. Boy, mine weren't any prizes. But Keith's, they didn't even want him. Neither of them . . . wow . . . rotten . . .

"Aw, come on. We're gonna give her a road test."

"I don't know, Pete . . ." I was thinking about June and wondering if maybe we could do both things. We had the whole day . . .

"Let me call June and ask her what she thinks."

"By the way, it's a convertible." Pete hung

up the phone without saying good-bye. He was really in a rush to hear from me so I dialed June's number right away.

"Boy, your mother gets worse and worse every time I get her on the phone," I told June when I finally got her mother to go and get June for me.

June's old lady was a real dippy dame. She got me on the phone like I was her long lost friend or something and would chew my ear off telling me stuff I didn't give a shit about hearing. I tried to be polite to her, but she sure made it tough.

"Today's one of her better days, too," June giggled. There wasn't anything she could do about her mother. She was getting out as soon as she went to college. That's why she worked so hard. She was stashing enough dough away to take care of herself just in case her folks decided they wouldn't put out for college for her.

"Hey, listen . . . how would you like to take a drive in an open convertible today?"

"Hmm . . . whose?"

"Pete told me Keith just got a new car from his old man and is taking it out for a road test." I had found a pencil in my mother's night table drawer and started doodling on a magazine lying on the table.

"Crazy Keith?" June knew about Keith. In a town like ours it was impossible not to get known if you were a nut like Keith.

"Yeah, but he's not really crazy." I said that

because I was feeling awful sorry for him just then.

"Who else is going?"

"Pete . . . I guess a couple of other guys . . . I don't know . . . anyhow it won't be too long a ride. It's a terrific day for a convertible too." I could feel the warm, sunny air licking my face and see June's hair blowing wild . . .

"Well, I was looking forward to our bike plans."

"We can do that, too," I rushed to tell her.

"Okay," she said and added, "give me a buzz when you're ready to pick me up."

"Okay." Then we talked for a while about things, like how we missed each other even though we saw each other just about every day. After a while I remembered Pete was waiting for my answering call. I always hated to say good-bye to June, even over the phone.

"It's gorgeous." That was the only word I could think of when I saw Keith's car. It must have cost Keith's old man a fortune. Keith was running his hand over the bright red enamel hood looking like he had blown his mind. I never saw him look so happy.

"How about the mileage?" Jerry, one of Keith's crazy buddies asked. Keith didn't have any close friends, not like Pete and me were to each other. He had buddies he ran around with but that was all. Just kicks, no serious stuff. I remember trying to be friendly a long time before, but Keith turned me off. He didn't insult me or anything, he just sort of blanked out so I didn't try after a while. He was a funny guy.

"Let's try it out." Pete was already in the backseat of the car.

Jerry and another guy I didn't know got into the front with Keith.

"First, we gotta pick up June," I told Keith as I got into the car next to Pete.

"Whatta we need her for?" Jerry said.

"That's Scott's girl. He never makes a move without her," Pete said, laughing in such a way he made it sound like a dirty crack. Maybe I should have socked him then, but instead I told him to bug off or I'd break open his head. He looked at my face and closed his mouth. *Underneath that nasty skin beats the heart of a chicken*, I thought to myself, glad that Pete was still easy to scare.

I sat in the middle between June and Pete after we picked her up. I wasn't going to take any chances of having Pete say some rotten thing to her without me hearing at least. It was queer the way Pete still hated June. And she hated him, too—not that I could blame her. He sure was lousy to her but in a sneaky kind of way. It was almost as if he wanted her himself and was flirting with her just the opposite of the way he should've . . . It seemed like people got more complicated as you got to know them better. At least my friends did.

I used to be able to figure everybody out—

like what they would do and say most of the time. But lately I was finding it was getting tougher. Like Pete. Now I thought I knew that guy inside and out. Sure he acted a lot like he used to, but there was a difference. I couldn't put my finger on it. But . . .

The car made a sharp right onto the highway and June pressed against me, pushing my thoughts out of my head. I put my arm around her shoulders and settled back to enjoy the ride.

I turned to see if Pete was enjoying himself, too. The end of his scarf was whipping around in the wind behind him halfway over the trunk of the car. The car was headed out toward the country and we had the sun behind our heads. It was great. The wind streaming against my face, pulling my skin tight back, making it hard to breath.

"Want a smoke?" Jerry handed his cigarette back toward Pete. Pete took a long, slow drag and smiled. Then he handed it over to me. Now Pete didn't smoke ordinarily and neither did I so I knew right away what was happening. I would have known sooner if we had been inside a closed car instead of one where the wind blew away everything, including the sweet smell of grass.

"No thanks," I shook my head and Pete handed the joint back to Jerry. I felt a poke in my left rib and looked down at June. Her face told me she wasn't happy. I knew why. June and I had talked about pot. Neither of us smoked the stuff. June was really down on it. Me, I figured it wasn't my business what my buddies did to themselves. They didn't bother me and I wasn't going to tell them what to do.

The second joint was making the rounds when Keith got in the act.

"Hey, man, what about me?" Keith took his hand off the wheel to grab for the cigarette Jerry was passing on to the guy next to him.

"Hey Keith, watch what you're doing," I shouted, but the wind swept my words backwards. The car swerved too close to the shoulder of the road to suit me before Keith got his hand back on the wheel. I tapped him on the shoulder and leaned forward to holler in his ear.

"Keith, you're driving too fast." And boy was he ever. I got a glimpse of the speedometer as I looked over his shoulder and it was reaching past 80.

"Crazy," Jerry shouted out to me like he loved it. I knew he was beginning to feel no pain. That didn't bother me though. What worried me, and I could feel June squirming around next to me, was Keith. He already had taken one too many drags on that butt and was beginning to drive like he was swaying to some inner sound.

"Hey Pete," I shouted in his ear, "this is getting pretty dangerous."

"Aw, don't be so chicken," Pete said to me. The silly grin on his face made me realize that he was going off too.

I knew then that I was going to have to do

something if June and I were going to get out of that car alive. Keith was crazy all the time but Keith on grass was more than I wanted to have driving me around. I was getting scared. These guys didn't know or maybe they didn't care what happened to them. But all of a sudden, for the first time in my life, I cared about what was going to happen to me enough to do something smart.

We had gone pretty far out of town but we were still on the main road. We had driven about ten miles already.

"Keith, let's turn around now. The car runs great." I hollered into his ear. But Keith didn't answer. At least he didn't make like he heard me at all.

By now June was whispering in my ear asking me to get those clowns to slow down and turn around. I could see she was as upset as I was. What really bugged me about the whole scene was the way Pete was acting. He was just as big a jerk as the rest.

"We're gonna get ourselves killed," I hollered as loud as I could, hoping one of them would listen. But it didn't matter. They were working on their third round when I decided what I had to do if June and I were going to get home in one piece.

It was my life and I wasn't going to let a bunch of stupid clowns take it away from me. Those whacked out weirdos could kill themselves if they wanted to but that wasn't for me or June. I had a lot to do before I got sprayed all over a highway by some stoned nuts.

"Keith," I squeezed his shoulder with my hand. "Stop the car for a minute, will you?"

"Whatdya want?" At least he answered me. I had bet my plan on that.

"I gotta take a leak." If I had told him I wanted to get out of the car for any other reason, I knew the ride could really blow up into my last trip. There wasn't any point trying to reason with them. It only made them crazier . . .

"Hee, hee, he gotta pee," the jerk in the middle of the front seat sang out in a voice high enough for us to hear.

My plan must've been a good one because sure enough the car started slowing down and Keith pulled it over to the shoulder of the road . . .

"Ya got thirty seconds," he said grinning wildly, "then we leave, ready or not."

I shoved June out of the car, which was easy because she had to get out so I could.

"Well so long, you guys," I said to them once we got out and I closed the car door. "Have a hell of a time."

"Whatsa matter with you, Scott, you crazy?" Pete asked, sorer than hell.

"Nothin's the matter with me, Pete. We just think it's a perfect day for a walk, that's all. Thanks for the ride, Keith," I smiled at him, and

Keith, the crazy nut, smiled back at me, revved up his car and took off, wheels spinning and the car rocking wildly over the road.

June and I stood watching until we lost sight of Pete's waving scarf.

I took June's hand and squeezed it. "Ready for a long walk?"

"It's a perfect day for it," she said, and smiled at me.

We started laughing and walking then. And suddenly with the sun in my eyes I could really see for the first time. I knew just what was going to happen to me and it was going to be great.